The Girl with the Silver Eyes

DON'T MISS THESE OTHER BOOKS BY
WILLO DAVIS ROBERTS

Baby-sitting Is a Dangerous Job
Caught!
Hostage
The Kidnappers
Megan's Island
Scared Stiff
Undercurrents
The View from the Cherry Tree

WILLO DAVIS ROBERTS

The Girl with the Silver Eyes

ALADDIN

new york london toronto sydney

ALADDIN
An imprint of Simon & Schuster Children's Publishing Division
1230 Avenue of the Americas, New York, NY 10020
First Aladdin hardcover edition July 1980
Copyright © 1980 by Willo Davis Roberts
All rights reserved, including the right of reproduction in whole or in part in any form.
ALADDIN is a trademark of Simon & Schuster, Inc., and related logo is a registered trademark of Simon & Schuster, Inc.
For information about special discounts for bulk purchases, please contact
Simon & Schuster Special Sales at 1-866-506-1949 or business@simonandschuster.com.
The Simon & Schuster Speakers Bureau can bring authors to your live event. For more information or to book an event contact the Simon & Schuster Speakers Bureau at 1-866-248-3049 or visit our website at www.simonspeakers.com.
Manufactured in the United States of America 0711 FFG
10 9
Library of Congress Cataloging-in-Publication Data
Roberts, Willo Davis.
The girl with the silver eyes.
Summary: A ten-year-old girl, who has always looked different from other children, discovers that she not only has unusual powers but that there are others like her.
[1. Psychokinesis—Fiction. 2. Science fiction.]
I. Title.
PZ7.R54465Gi
[Fic.]
80-12391
ISBN 978-0-689-30786-7 (hc)
ISBN 978-1-4424-2170-7 (pbk)

Dedicated to my own "Katie"
KATHLEEN LOUISE ROBERTS

The Girl with the Silver Eyes

I

KATIE sat on the small balcony of apartment 2-A, looking down over the front sidewalk. There was no yard, except for a narrow strip of grass between the parking lot and the street. Nowhere to play. Her mother had been concerned about that, for though there was a park two blocks away, she did not want Katie to go there alone.

So for the moment she sat on the balcony, looking through the iron bars that formed the sides of it, and watched the activity in the street.

Katie had always lived in the country, and she had liked that. This seemed interesting, however, and it was a nice street. It was wide and shaded with big trees, and most of the time there wasn't a lot of traffic. Except when people were going to work, of course, the way they were now.

She saw Miss Katzenburger emerge from the front door below and head toward the street. Katie hadn't met her yet, but she knew who she was. She'd seen

3

which apartment she went into—3-B, one floor up—and had looked at the nameplate beside the door.

Miss Katzenburger had red hair and was quite pretty. Katie admired pretty people, like Miss Katzenburger and her mother; she wasn't pretty herself. Even if she hadn't had to wear horn-rimmed glasses, she knew that her face was plain. Her hair was an ordinary color, a sort of pale tan that was not quite blonde and not quite brown, and as straight as it was possible for hair to be. When she grew old enough to have a choice, she thought she might like to be redheaded, like Miss K. Or, her second choice, blonde like her mother.

"Hey, Joy, wait a minute!"

Katie pressed her face against the cold bars to see who was calling after Miss K. Oh, *him*.

She *had* met Mr. Pollard. He lived in 3-A, right across from Miss K., and she'd collided with him on the stairs last night, her first whole day at The Cedars Apartments. He had dropped some papers he was carrying, and Katie had stepped on them, after which he had sworn at her. And then, when she had said nothing except, "I'm sorry," and stared at him, Mr. Pollard quickly snatched up his papers and edged around her, almost running the rest of the way down.

The way people often ran away from her, Katie thought. She'd wondered if it would be different in the city from the way it had been at home, near Delaney. Oh, they didn't always *run*, exactly, but when they looked into her face they often backed away, muttering things she couldn't understand, and hurried in some other direction.

Mr. Pollard, who was nearly bald on top even though he wasn't very old yet, didn't see her now. He caught

4

up with Miss K., and their voices carried clearly to the little balcony over their heads.

"I'm afraid I've missed my bus; could you give me a lift?" he asked.

"Sure," Miss K. agreed. She had a nice voice. "I have to pick up my girl friend, Angie, on the way."

"That's OK. Just so I get downtown. I had to stay up for hours last night, redoing all those papers that brat walked on, and I overslept."

Katie tightened her fingers on the bars. It had been just as much his fault as hers that they'd run into each other; he had been running, too. Why were so many things *her* fault?

They had stopped, just a few yards out from the front edge of the balcony; she could see the tops of their heads, one a beautiful mass of red-gold curls, the other with a few strands of hair combed across the bald spot.

"Wait a minute, have I got my keys?" Miss K. dug around in her handbag. "What brat are you talking about? The little girl in 2-A? I thought she looked like a cute little owl, with those glasses. The quiet type. I doubt if she'll be any trouble. Oh, here they are!"

Miss K. held the keys up, jingling them. Katie always thought of people by their initials; it was easier, especially when they had names like Katzenburger. Mr. P. shifted his briefcase to the other hand. "Did you look at her? At her eyes?"

Miss K. stopped jingling the keys. "No. What about them?"

"They're silver. And they're weird, she's a weird kid."

"Silver eyes?" Miss K. looked at him more closely. "Mr. Pollard, you haven't been drinking, have you?"

"Of course not! Look at the kid the next time you

see her—she's got funny eyes, I tell you! And I thought you were going to call me Hal."

They started walking toward the cars in the parking area. Miss K. owned a light blue Pinto; Katie had seen her get out of it yesterday afternoon.

They were almost there when Mr. P. gave a howl of mingled pain and rage, and doubled over, grabbing for his ankle. Then he turned and looked back toward the building.

His eyes met Katie's, and there was fear and anger in them. He swore again, loudly enough so she could hear it. "I told you, there's something strange about that kid. I nearly broke my ankle."

Miss K. stared at him in amazement. "Well, I can see that, but what did *she* have to do with it? You tripped over a rock!"

"Yeah! Yeah, I got hit in the ankle by a rock that wasn't there a few minutes ago. It just sort of . . . sort of slid right out in the middle of the sidewalk and smacked me!"

He was still glaring at Katie as he rubbed at his injured ankle, hopping on one leg, then balancing himself against a light post.

"Oh, for heaven's sake! You can't possibly be blaming a child for that?" Miss K. unlocked the car door and regarded him in exasperation.

"There wasn't any rock on the sidewalk a minute ago, was there? Did you see it, a minute ago? Did you ever see a rock on the sidewalk before?"

"Well, no," Miss K. admitted. "But they're all around the edges of the flower beds; something must have knocked one loose."

"What?" Mr. P. demanded. "What was near it? It

moved *just now*, just in time to connect with my ankle bone! And she's up there, watching us."

Miss K. lifted her gaze to the second floor balcony. For a moment their eyes locked over the distance between them. Katie's face didn't change expression. She could see Miss K. thinking it over, and then she said, "She's only a cute little girl."

"Cute? Are we talking about the same kid?" Mr. P. turned and stared at her too, angry and baffled. "I don't know how she does it, but there's something about her."

"Well, if you want a ride with me, come on," Miss K. said, and they got into the Pinto and drove away.

Katie sat watching two men from the apartment house across the street, men who didn't pay any attention to her. And then she remembered the rock that was still in the middle of the sidewalk, and she stared at it, very hard, until it began to move. It slid slowly at first, and then, as Katie's power built up with increased effort, it spurted off the rest of the way and lodged somewhat crookedly in the edge of the flowerbed.

Katie had known, long before she learned that by *thinking* about moving things she could actually *move* them, that she was different from other kids. She knew it partly because the adults around her *said* so.

She had lived with her mother and father until she was nearly four, and she remembered that, though they had both been kind and affectionate, they had sometimes been puzzled by her behavior.

"She never cries!" Monica Welker had said, on more than one occasion, when Katie was listening. "I didn't want a *fussy* baby, but even when she was only an infant, she never cried! At first I was terrified that there

7

was something wrong with her—mentally, I mean. It wasn't long before we could see *that* wasn't so—and then she went almost too far the other way. I mean, Katie's so *bright* that sometimes she frightens me!"

Katie, considering that, thought Monica rather confused. First she was afraid her baby was retarded, and then was equally afraid because she was intelligent.

She had, when she was little, called her parents Mama and Daddy. But now Monica didn't seem like her mother at all. Her parents had gotten a divorce when she was three, almost four years old, and her mother had gone to work and couldn't keep her, so she'd gone to live with Daddy and Grandma Welker. But then Daddy had gone away to work somewhere else, and she had lived with just Grandma; and Grandma, too, thought she was peculiar. While she lived with Grandma, Monica had come to see her sometimes, but it was clear Katie made her nervous.

Of course, part of that, Katie realized, was her own fault. When she knew that some of the things she did were things no other kid she'd ever met could do, maybe she should have stopped doing them. At least where other people could know about them, anyway. But it was like having an itch and not scratching it. When she wanted to move something, the compulsion was too strong to resist; usually, she'd already done it by the time she thought about the consequences.

Like the time her grandma had hurt her leg and was muttering about not wanting to leave her Social Security check in the mailbox for fear those nasty Johnson boys would steal it on their way home from school. They often went along peeking into everyone's boxes to see what was there, and more than once they'd scattered mail in the ditches beside the road.

"I don't think I can walk that far," Grandma Welker had said, rubbing at the knee she'd twisted when she slipped on the cellar steps.

"I could go get the check," Katie offered.

"No, no. I don't want you to go out there alone in this bad weather. You know what happened the last time."

The last time a man had stopped and asked her if she wanted a ride. He was a perfectly nice man, Katie knew he was, and she hadn't gotten into the car, and the man had simply smiled and driven away. Katie had tried to explain that it was only that he thought she was a long way from home, and it was cold and raining, and he was kind. But Grandma Welker was convinced he was a child molester.

Katie was a little vague about what child molesters actually *did*. But she knew it was something unpleasant, and she had sense enough not to get into a car or walk away with a stranger, for heaven's sake. Grownups told you and told you things, and then they acted as if you didn't have any brains at all, even when they admitted you were bright.

So, not wanting to upset her grandma, Katie had said no more. But when the old woman was busy peeling potatoes for supper, Katie sat in the window seat in the dining room and concentrated on the mailbox. The door of it stuck, and for a few minutes she thought it wasn't going to come open. But then it did, and she lifted the tan envelope that the government check always came in, wafted it noiselessly through the air, opened the door, brought it in, and deposited it on the dining room table.

Grandma Welker found it when she came in to set

the table. She let out a sort of yelp, like old Dusty when someone rocked on his tail, and almost dropped the plates she was carrying.

"Where did that come from?" she demanded.

Katie turned from the window seat, pulling her short skirt down over her knees to cover the scabs. "What?" she asked innocently.

"My check! My Social Security check!"

Katie simply stared at her blankly.

"Did the mailman bring it up to the house?"

"He must have," Katie decided, seeing an easy way out. Only her grandma couldn't leave it at that.

"Did he give it to you? Did he knock on the door?"

Katie stared. She knew it bothered the adults around her, the way she could keep her small face perfectly expressionless, yet it seemed the safest thing to do most of the time.

After a moment, her grandma gave up and took the check away, muttering under her breath.

Maybe, Katie thought, it would have been better to risk having the Johnson boys steal it than to have saved her grandma the walk to the mailbox.

It had taken her a while to learn to be careful about what she moved. She knew the name for the moving, now; she'd read it in a book. *Telekinesis.* That meant that she was able to move objects from one place to another without touching them. At first she hadn't realized that she was the only one who could do it. But when people got upset or excited about it, it didn't take her long to catch on.

There had been a time when Grandma Welker had been busy in the kitchen and had spoken to Katie over her shoulder. "I need a clean hanky. Be a good girl; run upstairs and get me one out of my top bureau drawer."

And Katie, who was curled in the rocking chair munching on an apple and reading *Call of the Wild*, paused long enough to slide open the bureau drawer, mentally search out the handkerchief, and waft the square of linen down the stairs and into Grandma's apron pocket.

"Katie! Did you hear what I said? Run upstairs—"

"There's a hanky in your pocket," Katie said, spitting out a seed and looking up long enough to see the amazement creep over her grandma's face when she felt in the apron pocket.

"Why, I declare, there wasn't one there a minute ago . . ."

She looked suspiciously at Katie, who was again engrossed in her book.

"I could see the edge of it sticking out," Katie said. Grandma Welker said no more, but the suspicion remained, unspoken.

As time went on, this peculiar ability of Katie's made more and more problems between them. When Katie learned how to turn off the light from the wall switch *after* she'd gotten into bed and turn the pages of her book without touching them (she didn't mean to do that when someone was watching her, but sometimes she forgot) and smooth her hair without using the hair brush, she made Grandma Welker nervous.

Grandma stopped taking her to church after the time the pages of Pastor Grooten's sermon got all mixed up, although Katie hadn't actually had anything to do with that. A breeze had come in the open window (it was a very hot day), and the pages had slithered off onto the floor, and when he picked them up they were out of order.

Of course, she *had* been responsible when Pastor Grooten's hair stood on end and seemed to do an odd little dance. It had been a long, boring sermon, and Katie, unable to keep her mind on it, had started entertaining herself. She hadn't thought anyone would notice. She'd also stirred up air currents carrying pollen from a nearby field of ragweed, and people in the congregation had begun to grab for their handkerchiefs.

Pastor Grooten was the sort of preacher who didn't appreciate crying babies during his sermons, nor coughing and sneezing. He had paused and looked down on his flock, frowning. How could all those people suddenly have to sneeze at the same time?

Just for the fun of it, Katie had shifted the air current then so that the pollen drifted under his own nose; and when he sneezed, Pastor Grooten had to grab for his sermon pages before they sailed off the lecturn. But they didn't actually slide until the next Sunday. On that day Katie remembered how suspicious her grandma had been about Pastor's hair standing on end the Sunday before (after the windows had been closed by one of the deacons). It all came to a head after the service when Grandma had said Katie could stay with old Mrs. Tanner, down the road, instead of going to church. Mrs. Tanner was bedridden, and Katie could read to her for an hour and a half a week, on Sunday mornings.

Katie didn't mind. She read very well—she had taught herself to read at the age of three—and Mrs. Tanner let her read anything she wanted to. Katie read her *Gentle Ben*, and *The View From the Cherry Tree*, and *Charlie and the Chocolate Factory*. And Mrs. Tanner fed her oatmeal cookies. They were store bought, and not as good as homemade, but it was a kind thought.

After those fateful Sundays, though she preferred the new arrangement, Katie knew she had to be more careful. She tried to lull Grandma Welker's suspicions by walking after things and not turning off the light from in bed unless she was sure her grandma was nowhere about.

It was too late, though. While Grandma Welker didn't come right out and accuse Katie of being a witch, or something worse, it was easy to see that she wasn't comfortable around her.

Mr. and Mrs. Armbruster, the neighbors across the road, made it clear that they didn't want Katie around *their* place. Most of the things they blamed on Katie were things she hadn't had a thing to do with, just like when the wind blew Pastor Grooten's sermon pages around. Things like ripe fruit dropping onto Mr. Armbruster's head could happen to anyone who walked through an orchard at the right time of year. If he hadn't seen Katie watching him at the time, would he have thought she had anything to do with it? And she hadn't been the one who opened the gate and let the pigs out into the cornfield that was supposed to be growing silage for Mr. Armbruster's cows.

The Armbrusters had never accused her of being a witch, either; but Mr. Armbruster did say (in Katie's hearing, to Pastor Grooten) that he always seemed to be unlucky when that child was around. Like so many of the people Katie saw regularly, the Armbrusters regarded her as someone to be mildly afraid of.

The same was true of the kids at school.

Katie knew she would never be the type who joined in and became a leader of anything. She *was* good at games, but there was always someone who didn't like the way she played them. She didn't like balls coming at her, hard and fast; once, when she was a kindergartener, she'd been hit in the face with a softball, and her glasses were broken and she'd had a black eye. That was before she learned how to make the ball veer off to one side. She knew that could spoil a game, but somehow, like other things she did, she couldn't help doing it. When it seemed vital to move something, she moved it.

So far, that rock she'd sent out to connect with Mr. P's ankle was the heaviest thing she'd moved. The power was growing stronger, she was certain of that. Maybe someday she'd be able to move big things, like automobiles or people.

Sitting there on the balcony of The Cedars Apartments, Katie giggled, thinking about moving Mr. P. suddenly up the stairs, with his briefcase and his papers flying in all directions. She'd never dare to do anything like that, but it was amusing to think about.

"Katie!" Monica's voice came through the open sliding glass doors behind her. Monica wanted Katie to call her *Mama*, the way she had when she was little, but so far Katie couldn't bring herself to do it. Grandma Welker had always referred to her as *Monica*, and that's what Daddy had called her, too, and Katie had come to think of her that way. She was, after six years of living apart, almost a stranger to Katie.

"Katie! Where are you? Oh—honey, be careful out there, it's a long way to the ground."

Monica stood in the opening, dressed for work in a smart summer suit of pale blue that made her eyes bluer and her hair more blonde. There was an anxious expression on her pretty face.

"How could I fall off, when I'm sitting down behind the bars?" Katie asked reasonably. "Are you ready to go?"

"Yes. The sitter just arrived. Come in and meet her, darling."

"I told you," Katie said. "I don't need a sitter. I'm almost ten years old, you know."

"Yes. But you're used to living in the country, and it's different, in the city. All kinds of things can happen—"

"I know about child molesters and all that," Katie said with dignity. "And keeping the doors locked, and not admitting on the telephone that I'm alone. I'm not *stupid*."

"No, of course not. But I'll feel better if there's someone here with you. So indulge your old mother, will you? And put up with her?"

Katie got up off the floor of the balcony and went inside, sighing. It was so silly, and a needless expense, too, to have a sitter for someone who was nearly ten. Especially when she knew Monica really couldn't afford it. She'd already admitted this apartment was the best she could manage, and she'd have to cut down on something else to pay for it.

Not that there was anything wrong with the apartment. It was very nice. Only it was small. Monica had been living in a one bedroom place, which was cheaper, and had had to find this one in a hurry when Grandma Welker died. Katie's bedroom was so little there was only room for a single bed, a dresser, and a tiny desk, but it was considered a two bedroom apartment. The pantry at Grandma's had been larger than Katie's new

15

bedroom. Some of the closets had been almost as large.

"Mrs. Hornecker, this is my daughter Katie," Monica was saying brightly. "Katie, this is the sitter, Mrs. Hornecker."

Katie took one look at Mrs. H. and knew she was going to hate her.

2

MRS. HORNECKER was tall and thin and had very large feet. She also had a wart on her chin with two hairs sticking out of it.

Katie stared at the wart, fascinated. She had never seen anything so ugly on a human face. "Does it hurt?" she asked.

Monica, her hand on the doorknob, paused to look back.

"Does what hurt?" Mrs. H. asked. She had a voice that sounded as if it were rising through gravel.

"The wart," Katie said.

Mrs. H.'s face got red, and Monica made a strangled sound.

"Katie, for pete's sake, it isn't polite to say things like that!"

Mrs. H. cleared her throat, but her voice still sounded gravelly. "You go on to work, Mrs. Welker. I'll handle the little girl."

Monica scuttled through the opening, glad to escape.

Mrs. H. stared down on Katie as if deciding whether to eat her fried or boiled.

"You're old enough to have better manners than that," Mrs. H. said. "To make remarks about things like warts."

"Are you supposed to give me lessons in manners?" Katie asked. "I think you were just hired to sit me. Which I don't need. I'm quite capable of taking care of myself."

"Let's get one thing straight right now," Mrs. H. told her. "I don't stand for no sass. Your ma said you were a little bit difficult, but I don't think you're any match for *me*."

Don't you? Katie thought. Well, they'd see about that. She suspected she was more than a match for Mrs. H., and she tried not to be hurt about Monica saying she was *difficult*. How was she difficult?

"Your ma said you ain't had your breakfast yet. I'll get it," Mrs. H. said and stomped on her enormous feet into the kitchen. "I believe in kids taking responsibilities," she said. "Suppose while I'm cooking, you set the table. I had to be here so early, I didn't eat yet, either, so set two places."

Katie said nothing. She stood in the doorway, not moving, while the sitter looked into the refrigerator. Mrs. H. got out eggs and butter and jam and a package of sausages, and then she opened the freezer and found a can of frozen orange juice. After a few minutes she turned crossly from what she was doing to say, "I told you to set the table, miss."

"It's set," Katie said. Her eyes had a silvery gleam behind her glasses, and she knew it was true that she did look rather like an owl with those horn-rims.

"You ain't moved from that spot . . ." Mrs. H. began,

and then stopped. For the table had two plastic plates, juice glasses, and silverware on it. For the first time the sitter seemed uncertain. "You forgot the napkins," she said, though not as if they mattered very much. Katie could almost see the workings of the sitter's mind, wondering how she'd managed to set the table without moving. "Your ma set the table before she left?"

Katie didn't answer. She'd learned it was disconcerting to grownups if you didn't answer. She waited until Mrs. H. reached out with a fork to turn the sausages, then whisked a pair of paper napkins from the holder on the counter to a place beside each plate.

One of them was still moving when the sitter turned toward Katie and the Formica topped table.

Mrs. H. swallowed and dropped the fork. It didn't fall onto the floor, however, but drifted slowly toward the counter and came to a rest beside the electric frying pan.

All the color washed out of Mrs. H.'s face, and Katie watched a tremor begin at her lips and then spread to her hands.

For a moment neither of them spoke. Katie's small face was blank. She knew perfectly well she was taking a risk, but the idea of having Mrs. H. for a sitter all summer, until it was time to go back to school, was more than she could bear. She had to get rid of her at once, today.

Mrs. H. moistened her lips. "Where you been?" she asked carefully. "These years you weren't living with your ma?"

"Locked up, mostly," Katie said. It was partly true. Grandma Welker had taken to locking her in at night, sometimes, until she found out that it didn't work, that somehow the key would turn in the lock, or the bar would slide back, even if they were not within Katie's reach but on the other side of the door.

Mrs. H. was very pale. She'd forgotten about eating.

Katie, however, was hungry. She decided not to overdo things by causing the sausages and eggs to come to her across the kitchen, so she walked over and got her own, leaving some for the sitter. Besides, she was afraid the loaded plate might be too heavy for her to hold in the air and would fall on the floor.

She had forgotten to bring the toast, however; it popped up just as the telephone rang. Mrs. H. turned her head, and the toast leaped out of the toaster and sailed across the kitchen. Mrs. H. would not have noticed except that one slice missed its mark; instead of landing on Katie's plate, it hit the edge of the table and fell with a little scuffling sound to the floor.

The telephone continued to ring, and Mrs. H. fled to answer it.

Katie ate her breakfast, all of it, and the sitter had not yet come back. She wondered if she ought to let well enough alone, or if something more was needed to assure that Mrs. H. would not return tomorrow.

She decided to wait and see what happened. In the meantime, she would find out if there was anyone in the swimming pool. She'd been told she must not ever swim unless there was someone with her. She tried to picture Mrs. H. in a bathing suit, and her usually solemn face cracked in a grin.

The little balcony in front was a private one, not connected to the one for 2-B. However, there was a railed deck that ran around the inside of the building, overlooking the pool, and everyone in the apartment had access to that. Katie went out onto the deck and stood looking down into the bright blue water.

There was no one swimming. She hadn't really thought there would be, this time of day, although it was already getting quite hot in the sun. She wondered if there were any kids living here besides herself. She'd asked Monica when she arrived, night before last, but Monica had only lived there herself for a week. She didn't know anybody yet.

Katie sat down, cross-legged, Indian fashion, on the warm boards of the deck. Maybe if she waited someone would decide to swim. Or at least come out onto the deck so she could see who lived here and what they looked like.

She couldn't imagine living here a week and not knowing anybody. It was certainly going to be different from living in the country near a little town like Delaney. Here she wouldn't be able to go for long walks by herself and make the leaves in the fall swirl up like a cloud of brightly colored smoke and talk to herself without having everybody think she was crazy. The kids called her that, sometimes. Crazy Katie.

Why should it be crazy to talk to yourself? Who else were you going to talk to, if you didn't have any friends?

Katie didn't think it was peculiar, but she didn't like the way people looked at her when she talked to herself, so she only did it when she was alone. Or thought she was alone. Around here, she'd feel as if someone were watching and listening all the time, behind the sliding glass doors and the drawn draperies. All of them were drawn except her own, behind her.

Through the sliding doors she'd left half open, she heard Mrs. H.'s voice on the telephone. "Well, you tell her to call home as soon as she gets in, please."

So she was calling Monica already. Katie wriggled a little, uneasily, wondering if Mrs. H. would tell Monica exactly what had happened, or if she'd simply quit. She hoped she'd just quit. As often happened after she'd given in to the temptation to shake someone up a bit, Katie was now having second thoughts. Maybe she shouldn't have been so obvious about the things she did, just to frighten the sitter off. Maybe, one of these days, someone who was grownup would decide she *was* crazy, and they'd really lock her up. In a place where she couldn't manipulate the locks and get loose.

The thought made her cold, and she rubbed at the goosebumps that rose on her bare arms.

Monica had driven up to Delaney to get her the day before yesterday, Saturday, coming to the Tanner's where Katie had slept in the spare room ever since Grandma Welker had died. Mrs. Tanner, who was half-blind and more than half-deaf, didn't think there was anything peculiar about Katie. You could run the shades up and down, turn the lights on and off, adjust the volume or change the channel on TV, or let the pages of the book on your lap turn themselves, and Mrs. Tanner didn't even notice. So when Monica asked rather nervously how they'd been getting along, Mrs. Tanner smiled and said just fine, she and Katie always got along, and she was sure going to miss Katie's reading.

Monica had seemed relieved at that, and said no, they didn't have time to stay for supper; they had a long drive and they'd better go right away. She'd loaded Katie's belongings into the Celica, and crammed Katie in between things, and they'd taken off for the city. Katie had paused only long enough to pat old Dusty's doggy head. There was a lump in her throat, so she didn't say anything. Old Dusty was probably too deaf to hear her, anyway.

They stopped on the way for hamburgers with onions and french fries and milkshakes. Katie had pineapple and Monica had vanilla.

It wasn't easy to talk to Monica. Katie told herself that since Monica was her mother, they ought to love each other, especially now if they were going to live together again.

She didn't feel like loving Monica, though. How could you not resent the fact that your mother had given you to someone else to raise, instead of keeping you herself?

Monica tried to explain, of course. "It wasn't that I didn't want you, honey. You know that, don't you? I've told you before, it was because I had to work and I couldn't take care of you when you were little. When your daddy and I were together, why, then we at least made enough money to pay for a sitter. Or, most of the time, Daddy worked one shift and I worked another one, and we took care of you between us. But I just couldn't do it after Daddy left."

Monica glanced at her quickly, driving along the highway, but Katie didn't look back. Her hair was blowing in the wind, and it felt good and cool on her hot cheeks. She pretended to be interested in a herd of Holstein cows grazing in a field, although she'd seen plenty of cows. She supposed there wouldn't be any where they were going.

"I always wished," Monica said, "that I didn't have to live so far away from you, so that I could come and visit you more often. I *did* miss you, Katie."

Katie said nothing, and after that Monica didn't talk

much the rest of the way. That was until just before they got there, when she suddenly cleared her throat the way grownups did when they were telling you things for your own good. So far, Katie hadn't seen that it really *was* for her own good, but that's what they often said.

"You'll meet Nathan tomorrow," Monica said. "He's a good friend of mine. He'll probably come over tomorrow."

Katie hadn't expected that. She turned her head so quickly that it hurt her neck. "Does he live there?"

Monica turned pink. "No. He's just a good friend. But he'll be there a lot."

Katie's alarm subsided, not all the way, but a little. She was glad this Nathan wasn't going to live with them. She was uncomfortable about the idea of her mother having a boyfriend, though. She knew that was what they called them, even though they were grown men. She'd heard the kids at school talking about their mother's boyfriends, or their father's girl friends. Most of them would rather have lived with parents who were married to each other, but they were resigned to not being able to. Kids had to resign themselves to all kinds of things they didn't really like.

When they got to the apartment, it was late, and they went right to bed and slept late the next morning. By the time they'd had a late breakfast, Nathan was there. He was a big man with dark hair and dark eyes and a brushy dark beard. He grinned at Katie and said, "Hi, kid."

"Good afternoon," Katie said. She had looked around for signs that Nathan spent a lot of time there, and then remembered that Monica had only been there herself for a week, so nothing looked quite lived-in yet. There was a pack of cigarettes beside an ashtray on the coffee table, though, and Nathan lit one of them. Katie hated tobacco smoke, and she edged away from him.

Nathan looked at Monica and rolled his eyes. "Get her. *Good afternoon*." He mimicked Katie's solemn words. "Is this your kid or your mother?"

"Stop it," Monica said. "Let Katie be herself."

Who else could she be, Katie wondered. She walked around the living room, peering through the sliding glass doors to see the pool on one end—which looked interesting—and the balcony and the parking lot on the street side. There was one bookcase, and Katie pushed her glasses up on her nose without touching them and looked at the titles. Monica's tastes ran to romances and thrillers. Well, Katie found romances rather boring, unless they had a lot of swashbuckling action in them, with sword fights or gun battles. But some of the thrillers weren't bad. She took out a book with a bright red cover, titled *The Secret of Fire House Five*, and hadn't even opened it yet when Monica swooped it out of her hands.

"I don't think that one's appropriate for someone your age, honey. There's a branch library four blocks over; you can get some suitable material there. I'll take you next Saturday."

If it was only four blocks, Katie didn't see any need to wait a week to get something to read. She wondered what was in the red book that wasn't appropriate and resolved to find out as soon as Monica went to work on Monday.

Nathan collapsed in a big chair and blew smoke in

Katie's general direction. "How about a beer?" he suggested. He slung one leg over the chair arm and put the other foot on the coffee table.

Nathan wouldn't have lasted five minutes in Grandma Welker's house. Katie shifted the air current so that the smoke floating toward her turned back and surrounded Nathan's head like a miniature cloud.

Monica brought the beer and offered Katie a glass of lemonade. It wasn't homemade, but it tasted pretty good. Katie moved farther away from the cloud of smoke and went on looking for something appropriate in the bookcase. After a minute Nathan said, "For pete's sake, open a window or something. It sure is stuffy in here."

"Is it all right if I take this in my room and read?" Katie asked, holding up a paperback titled *The Unicorn Girl*.

"Sure, honey," Monica agreed quickly. "Unless you want to sit out here with us and watch TV."

"I don't watch much TV," Katie told her. "I can make up better stories in my head than most of those silly things."

She walked toward the door of the small room that was now hers and heard Nathan's voice behind her. "What kind of kid is this one of yours, Monica? I never saw one like her before."

He didn't lower his voice. He was one of those people who talk about kids as if they weren't there or couldn't hear. Of course, it was probably true that he'd never seen anyone like Katie. She hadn't met anyone else like herself, either. She wished, quite sincerely, that she *would*.

It was lonely, being the only one like herself.

"I never saw eyes that color," Nathan said behind her.

26

"Nothing like yours. Did your husband have silver eyes?"

"They're not silver," Monica said uneasily. "They are just gray. No, Joe had brown eyes."

"Isn't it genetically unlikely that a brown-eyed person and a blue-eyed person would have a kid with silver eyes?"

"*Gray* eyes," Monica insisted.

Katie closed the door so she couldn't make out their words any more. She sprawled on the bed that felt hard and unfamiliar beneath her and opened *The Unicorn Girl*.

To her intense disappointment, it wasn't about a girl unicorn at all, it was only about a girl who could *talk* to unicorns. Well, maybe it would still be worth reading. It would be fun to be able to talk to unicorns, Katie thought.

At least it would be better than talking to herself.

3

N o o n e came to swim in the pool all morning.

After a while Katie got tired of sitting there looking at the empty swimming pool. She discovered that if she concentrated very hard, she could make the water splash up over the edge and run in rivulets back over the tile. Someone had left their shoes and socks beside a deck chair, and she leaned forward and tried *very* hard, until the water rushed over the edge of the pool in a wave sufficient to wet the shoes and socks.

Nobody came and found them, however, and Katie got up and began to walk around the deck. There were no name cards beside the doors on this inner courtyard, and all the draperies were drawn so that she couldn't see inside. She thought living at The Cedars Apartments was going to be pretty boring.

There was a plain door sandwiched in between the sliding glass doors; and when Katie opened it, she found herself in a short corridor that led out to the main one.

Well, maybe she'd give herself a tour of this floor, at least, since she didn't want to go back to 2-A. Not while Mrs. H. was there.

The card beside the bell of 2-B said *Michaelmas*. No Mr. or Mrs., just the last name. And in front of the door sat a cat.

He was a big gray tom with a few black marks on his face that gave him an evil look, and he crouched there in a position that made Katie drop to her knees before him.

"What's the matter, cat? You look sick."

I am sick. I hurt.

Surprise held her rigid. The cat hadn't spoken to her, of course, he hadn't. Yet the words hung in her mind, as clearly as if she'd heard them.

"Where do you hurt?" She didn't touch him, only hunkered down so that they were face-to-face. He had yellow, unblinking eyes.

The door opened so unexpectedly that Katie nearly fell over.

"Oh, there you are, Lobo—well, who're you?"

The lady who stood in the doorway—Mrs. Michaelmas?—was as old as Grandma Welker had been. She wore a red and green and blue printed muumuu in electric colors, and her white hair hadn't been combed yet today. (Later she would learn that Mrs. Michaelmas's hair never looked as if it had been combed.)

"I'm Katie Welker. I live over there." She gestured at the door of 2-A.

"Well, glad to know you. I'm Annie Michaelmas. And that wretched creature," she pointed at the cat, "is Lobo. Lobo means—"

"Wolf," Katie supplied.

29

"Oh, you speak Spanish?"

"I can read a few words of it," Katie said modestly. "Lobo is sick. He hurts."

"He does?" For once a grownup didn't act as if she were crazy or weird. Mrs. M. bent to pick him up, and Lobo struggled in her arms. "Where do you hurt, baby?"

"I think it's a bladder infection. Bladder infections really hurt. My grandma had one once."

"I did, too. And you're right. They hurt." She cradled the cat against her brightly flowered bosom. "I guess I better take him to the vet's, eh?"

"I think so." Katie could see beyond Mrs. M. into a comfortably cluttered apartment. There were books and magazines all over it, in shelves and on tables and even on the floor. Her interest quickened.

"I don't suppose you'd lend me something to read, would you, until I can go to the library? Monica—my mother—says her books aren't suitable for a ten-year-old."

Mrs. M. looked down at her nearsightedly. "Are you ten? Well, I guess we can't all be giants, can we. Sure, I can lend you something. What do you like? True detective stories? Science fiction? Murder mysteries?"

Katie nodded. "Anything, as long as it's good."

"Come on in and look around. What's your name?" Mrs. M. asked.

Katie told her, and followed her into the apartment. There was a television, but there were newspapers lying on top of it and over the edge so that they covered up part of the screen. She guessed that Mrs. M. spent more time reading than watching TV.

"Make yourself at home," Mrs. M. said, depositing Lobo gently on a couch with orange and brown flowers on it. "I'll call and ask when Dr. Grant can see Lobo. You hungry? I got some nice fruit there on the table. Help yourself."

Katie selected a bunch of purple grapes and walked between a big shabby leather recliner and a chair with blue and green stripes and a red pillow in it, to reach the bookshelves.

Behind her, Mrs. M.'s voice boomed. "Four o'clock? OK, I'll be there."

She turned back, running a hand over Lobo's drooping head. "We'll take care of you, baby. Don't you worry, my friend. You find anything to read?"

Katie assumed that last question was directed at her, unless Lobo was better educated than she thought he was.

"I'm still looking. What's a Pimpernel?"

"*The Scarlet Pimpernel?* You never read that? That's one of the best books anybody ever wrote," Mrs. M. told her. "You take that one along; you'll like it. I'll bet I've read it twenty times. Maybe more."

Katie accepted the book and sucked a grape out of its skin, swallowing the two parts separately. "When I finish this, can I come back and get something else?"

"Sure, why not. Listen," Mrs. M. said, "I know how it is at the vet's. I'll sit there for half an hour and just when it's my turn to take Lobo in somebody'll bring in their St. Bernard for emergency major surgery and I'll have to wait another hour or two. The paper boy comes to collect tonight, if he's on schedule. Will you watch for him and pay him? I got the money right here. He usually comes about five."

"OK," Katie agreed, accepting the bills.

"Name's Jackson Jones," Mrs. M. told her. "And he's a tall, skinny kid with one blue eye and one green one.

31

You can't mistake him."

"Really?" That sounded even more peculiar than having silver eyes, having one blue and one green. "All right, I'll watch for him."

"When you finish *The Scarlet Pimpernel*," Mrs. M. said, "try this one." She put another book into Katie's hand. "You like westerns? Louie L'Amour?"

Katie decided she liked Mrs. M. as much as she disliked Mrs. H. And since it was getting on toward lunchtime and the grapes weren't quite enough to stave off her hunger pangs, she decided she'd better go home.

She had to go back out on the inner courtyard deck and in through the sliding glass doors because the front door was locked and she didn't have a key. She jumped when Mrs. H. spoke from the kitchen; somehow she'd hoped the sitter would just leave, even if that wasn't an ethical thing for a sitter to do.

"Where have you been?"

Katie shrugged. "Around."

"Well, suppose you take yourself into your bedroom and make up your bed. You're big enough to be responsible for that."

Had the woman decided that she'd imagined the things that had happened earlier? Had she talked to Monica and quit, or had she changed her mind? Maybe, Katie thought, she ought to make sure Mrs. H. didn't have second thoughts about staying on in this job. She didn't even have to concentrate very hard to smooth the sheets on her bed, and then the blanket, and finish up with the spread. She couldn't shift the pillow as well as she'd have liked, so it was left crooked, but not much.

Mrs. H. was getting angry when Katie just stood there with what she took to be a stubborn look on her face.

"I'm here through today," she said in a harsh voice, "and while I'm here, you'll do as you're told. Straighten up your room."

"It's straightened," Katie said, and mentally whisked up a Kleenex and deposited it in the wastebasket.

"I looked in there ten minutes ago," the sitter said, "so don't tell me any lies."

"Why don't you look in there now?" Katie asked, and walked past the woman and into the living room. She would have liked to sit in the big leather chair, but it smelled of tobacco from when Nathan sat there, so she chose a smaller platform rocker.

She heard Mrs. H.'s heavy footsteps, as the woman peered into the doorway of Katie's bedroom, and then had to look up from the book she had just opened when Mrs. H. towered over her.

There was something menacing about her. Katie's heartbeat quickened; what would she do if Mrs. H. touched her? Could she stop the woman from hitting her?

"How do you do it?" the sitter asked.

"Do what?" Katie assumed the air of injured innocence that had so baffled and frustrated her grandma, her teachers, and the other adults around her.

For a moment more Mrs. H. stood there, then she turned and marched out of the room. Katie heard her in the kitchen. She wished she'd been there to overhear what the sitter had said to Monica on the phone. She assumed Mrs. H. had quit and wouldn't be back tomorrow.

Katie was so absorbed in *The Scarlet Pimpernel* that she forgot to watch the time. She had seen Mrs. M. go out, carrying Lobo in a cardboard cat-box, on their way to the veterinarian's. She was wearing a wine and pink and red flowered dress and carrying a gigantic white purse. And then Katie became so deeply immersed in the book—"It's like you were drugged or something, you don't even know what's going on around you," Grandma Welker used to say in annoyance about Katie's reading—that when the doorbell rang she jumped a foot.

Drat! She'd forgotten she'd promised Mrs. M. to watch for Jackson Jones, the paper boy. And she wanted to see his different colored eyes.

Mrs. H., who had stayed in the kitchen reading a *True Confessions* all day, got up, but Katie beat her to the door. She saw, guiltily, that it was past five, and she hadn't watched for the paper boy at all.

She hadn't missed him, though.

He did have one blue eye and one green one, although you probably wouldn't notice it right away unless you were looking for it. He was quite tall, and skinny, and he stared at her uncertainly.

"Mr. Redmond here? I'm collecting for the paper."

"No Mr. Redmond lives here," Katie told him. "My mother moved in a week ago."

He said a word that Katie had once said and had her mouth washed out with soap for it. "This is always happening to me," he said. "People move away without paying their bill. That's why I try to collect from most of 'em every week instead of by the month. There are so many cheats."

"Did he owe you very much?" Katie asked in sympathy.

"Four dollars and a half," Jackson Jones said. She guessed he was three or four years older than she was, though it was hard to tell for sure. He was so tall, and she was so small. "You people want to take the paper?"

"I don't know. I'll ask my mother when she comes home. I can tell you next time you come around."

The boy sighed. "Oh, I'll come around again tomorrow, probably. There's one guy in this building always makes me come back at least three or four times before he pays me. Mr. Pollard. He lives upstairs, in 3-A."

"I've met him. He's a real jerk," Katie agreed.

"He's not the only one on my route, but he's one of the worst. He used to say he didn't have the right change; and then when I started carrying some, he hadn't cashed his check, or only had a fifty dollar bill, or something. Well, I'll check tomorrow and see if your mother wants the paper."

"Oh! I almost forgot!" Katie dug into her pocket for the money the neighbor across the hall had given her. "This is from Mrs. Michaelmas. She had to take Lobo to the vet, and she asked me to pay you."

He took the money and wrote out a receipt. "She's a nice old lady, Mrs. Michaelmas is."

"She lent me some books. There don't seem to be any other kids in the building to play with, so I'm glad to have something to read."

"Nah, there's no other kids. I'm surprised they let you in here. People hate kids these days. They keep them out of most of the best places. Good thing we got our own house and don't have to rent, my Pa says. We got seven kids. Nobody'd rent to a family with seven kids."

Katie felt a surge of envy. "I don't have any brothers or sisters. Is it fun?"

Jackson Jones stopped writing on his pad and stared at her in amazement. "Fun? To have three sisters and

35

three brothers? You gotta be kidding!"

Katie knew Mrs. H. was standing where she could hear them, and she moved into the corridor and closed the door behind her before she remembered that that would make it lock and she didn't have a key.

"What's it like, then?"

"Being in a big family? It's like a madhouse. We got two bathrooms, but you can hardly ever get into one of 'em. Two of my sisters are fifteen and eighteen, and it takes them an hour apiece just to get ready to go to school in the morning. And I have to share a room with my brother Wally; he's seventeen, and he's an absolute slob. He leaves his pop bottles and his apple cores around until they grow mold, and he always has the light on when I want it off, and the other way around. He borrows my socks and underwear because he forgets to put his in the hamper so they never get washed. And nobody ever gets an allowance because Pa says with seven kids it's all he can do to keep us fed, so everybody has to earn his own spending money. That's hard to do when people won't pay you after you've done the work. Here, this is Mrs. Michaelmas's receipt. I let hers go for a month if she wants me to, because she never makes up excuses why she can't pay me. What's the matter with Lobo?"

"He has a bladder infection."

"Oh. Well, I hope he's gonna be OK. He's a good cat." Jackson Jones leaned forward to look at the new card Monica had inserted in the holder beside the door. "Your name's Welker?"

Katie nodded. "I'm Katie. Mrs. M. already told me your name—Jackson Jones. Do they call you Jack for short?"

He shook his head. "Nope. Even my mother calls me

Jackson Jones, practically all the time. 'Jackson Jones, I told you to clean up the basement!' or 'Jackson Jones, don't you dare put your feet on that clean bedspread.' That kind of thing. Well, it's time old Pollard was coming home. Maybe if I catch him out on the sidewalk, he can't pretend he doesn't hear me ringing his bell."

"Good luck," Katie said, and then she had to ring her own bell so that Mrs. H. would let her in.

No matter what Jackson Jones said, she'd bet it was more fun to be a member of a family than to be an only child. Maybe if you had brothers and sisters, they wouldn't think you were so peculiar they didn't want anything to do with you. And at least there'd be people around; it wouldn't be so lonely.

She had left her book lying open in the chair, but she didn't immediately return to it. Instead, she walked to the little front balcony, to see if Jackson Jones had any luck with Mr. P.

Mr. P. was there, all right. He'd just walked from the bus stop at the corner, and he was hot and perspiring. Katie heard Jackson's voice before she saw him as he came out of the front door below.

"Hello, Mr. Pollard. Could I collect for the paper? You owe me for two weeks, now."

"Not right now, kid, I'm in a hurry. I've got a date, and I'm going to be late for it. Come back tomorrow, OK?"

He brushed past Jackson Jones, who stared after him in mingled anger and frustration.

Katie couldn't see what happened, but she knew. She heard the front door slam in a sudden gust of wind—she used everything she could to build up the force of that wind—and Mr. P. swore and stumbled backward. If she craned her neck, at the end of the balcony she could see the top of his head, bald except for the strands of hair carefully combed across it. He was holding a hand to his face and blood spurted over the hand and dripped onto the sidewalk.

"Gee," Jackson Jones said. "You OK, Mr. Pollard? Did it break your nose?"

Mr. Pollard had to put down his briefcase to dig out a handkerchief, with which he staunched the bloody flow. He spoke indistinctly through the handkerchief. "What made the door blow shut? There isn't even any wind."

"Just a freak gust, I guess. Listen, Mr. Pollard, everybody else has paid me, and it would really save me some time if you could give me the money now. If you don't want to wait for the receipt, I could put it in your mailbox."

"I told you, I'm in a hurry." Mr. Pollard bent to retrieve his briefcase and hurried inside, slamming the door behind him.

Jackson Jones scowled after him, then glanced up and saw Katie on the balcony. "See? I told you."

"He's a jerk, all right," Katie agreed.

Jackson Jones got on his bike and rode off down the street, and Katie went back into the apartment. From inside the front door, she could hear Mr. Pollard's feet pounding on the stairs. Opening the door a crack, she watched as he rounded the top of the flight to the second floor and started up to the third.

She wondered if his briefcase opened only with a key, or if it was one of those cheap ones that had little clasps. She thought she could manipulate those things, so that the briefcase would pop open . . .

She heard Mr. P. start cursing before the cascade of

papers came sliding behind him down the stairs. Miss K was just coming up from the ground floor when he reached the second floor landing; both of them saw Katie, standing in her own doorway, and Mr. P. gave her a look that was sheer hatred.

"Good heavens," Miss K. said. "What happened to your nose?"

"The door blew shut on it," he said, sounding muffled as he bent over to scoop up his papers. "And then the catch broke on my case."

"Here, let me help you." Miss K. stooped to pick up the papers nearest to her. They looked as if they might be insurance policies. "Does it hurt very much?"

"It hurts like the devil. I don't suppose you could spare any ice, could you? So it won't swell so badly?"

"Sure, I can let you have some ice." Miss K. glanced toward Katie and smiled.

"Good. I'd appreciate it. Listen, are you busy tonight? For dinner? I don't know how this is going to look when I get it cleaned up, but if I'm not too much of a mess, would you like to join me? I thought maybe that little Italian place over on Third Street . . ."

They were moving away from her, up the stairs, and Katie didn't hear what Miss K. said to that.

But it had been a lie, what Mr. Pollard had said to Jackson Jones. He wasn't in a hurry for a date at all. Mr. Pollard was an awful liar.

She remembered the way he'd looked at her, as if he somehow knew she was responsible both for his bloody nose and his spilled briefcase.

She wondered if Mr. P. was dangerous.

4

M A Y B E Nathan didn't live with them, but he was sure there a lot. He came within ten minutes of the time Monica got home from work, carrying a six pack of beer and a bag of groceries, arriving just in time to say good-bye to Mrs. H. as she left.

Mrs. H. hadn't said anything. Only (tight-lipped and grim) that she didn't think she cared for the job, after all, and if Mrs. Welker could write her a check for today's wages, they'd call it quits.

"But why?" Monica asked. "What happened?"

"Let's just say your little girl and I don't exactly hit it off," Mrs. H. said, and the look she gave Katie was very much like the one Mr. P. had sent in her direction a few minutes earlier.

Maybe Mrs. H. thought if she told the truth everyone would think *she* was crazy. Anyway, Katie sighed in re-lief as the sitter vanished out the front door.

Monica didn't let it go at that, of course. "What did you *do*, Katie?"

40

Katie put on her blank face. "I read most of the day. I watched to see if anyone swam in the pool, so I could, too, but nobody did."

"I mean to Mrs. Hornecker! You must have said something, done something, to upset her. She called the office before I'd even had time to get there!"

Katie shrugged. "I don't need a sitter, anyway. I'm old enough to take care of myself."

"Katie, what did you *do?*"

Nathan breezed in then—Katie noted that he had a key—and looked at their faces. "What's going on?"

"The sitter quit. Early this morning she called me at the office to tell me to find someone else, she wasn't staying. And Katie won't say what happened."

Nathan stowed things in the refrigerator and added his frown to Monica's. "Well, kid, what have you got to say?"

Resentment formed a tight knot in her stomach, although Katie's face didn't change. Who was he to get tough with her?

"My name's Katie," she told him. "Not *kid*."

Nathan's ears turned pink. "Now, listen, you little—"

Monica put a hand on his arm. "No, Nathan, stop. Come on, let's get dinner. I'm hungry, you're hungry, we're all tired. Katie and I will talk later. I picked up a paper on the way home; I'll go through the ads after we eat and see if I can line up another sitter." She fixed a look on Katie that stopped a protest. "And don't tell me you don't need one. I'll have to be the judge of that."

"If you get another one," Katie observed, "she probably won't like me, either. Nobody does."

"Why not?" Monica demanded, forgetting what she'd said about waiting until after dinner. "You must say or

41

do something, Katie, to make people not like you!"

"I don't have to do anything. They just look at me, and they don't like me. They say I have peculiar eyes. I can't help it what color my eyes are, can I?"

She walked away, hoping Monica wouldn't think to call her back to do anything in connection with dinner, and heard Nathan mutter, "See? Other people notice it, too. She has got peculiar eyes, Monica."

Katie got her book and retreated with it to her own room. It was hard to concentrate on it, though, when she could hear their voices in the kitchen. Finally she didn't even try to read any more—*The Scarlet Pimpernel* was too good to ruin by reading it with half her attention—and she laid the book down and crept to the doorway.

She could make out their words, then, if she strained a little.

"Monica, there's more to this than you've said. I know there is. You were jumpy before you went up there to get the kid, and now you're a nervous wreck. What did you know, before you brought her back here? What's wrong with her?"

Monica sounded as if she were on the verge of crying. "I don't know. Honestly, Nathan, I don't! She's always been—well, different."

"How? Here, give me that, I'll tear up the lettuce; you get the steak. How is she different? Besides those funny eyes?"

"Well, when she was a baby, she never cried. I mean *never*, Nathan! Not when she was hungry or wet or I stuck her with a pin! She simply did not cry. And I asked Mother Welker once, a couple of years ago, if Katie ever got so she cried, and she said *no*. Whoever heard of a child who doesn't cry when she hurts herself, or any time?"

Katie leaned against the doorframe, listening to the clatter of silverware and plastic plates being slapped on the table.

"And you never could tell what she was thinking by her face. Her face shows *nothing*. Besides not crying, she doesn't laugh, either. Not around me, anyway. Oh, I know she resents the fact that I let her go live with Joe's mother; she thinks I deserted her, though I've tried to explain to her why I had to leave her. She'll be ten in September, and I'd think that would be old enough to understand something of what I've said, but she doesn't seem to."

"She doesn't want to," Nathan guessed.

"Maybe so. Nathan, it was so difficult. Even when I was married to Joe, and we both worked, there was never enough money to go around. We ran up all those medical bills, the year before Katie was born. I had a miscarriage after we were in a car accident, and neither of us worked for a month or more, and it was horrible. And then I got the job at Curtis Pharmaceuticals—I had to get a new job because they wouldn't hold my other one open until I could go back to work again—and things were better for a while. The wages were good, and the girls I worked with were nice and friendly—I still write to a couple of them—and it seemed as if we were going to get straightened out, financially."

Katie heard the controls *tick* as Monica turned on the broiler to preheat for the steaks, then Monica's clicking heels as she walked back to the sink.

"We wanted a baby, of course, and I was so pleased when I got pregnant again within six months. Joe and I

43

weren't having any trouble between us yet, then, and he wanted the baby, too. It was funny . . ." Monica made a little hiccuping sound, more sad than amused. "We joked about it, at work, that maybe the drugs we were handling had some magical powers, because four of us got pregnant almost at the same time. And then I had a difficult time with the pregnancy, and Joe and the doctor decided I'd better quit working until after Katie was born. I was hoping to go back to that job with Curtis—I *had* to work, Joe just didn't make enough to keep us going and pay all the bills, which was part of the problem we had that broke us up, I suppose—but they ended it, about a month after I left."

"Ended what?" Nathan asked.

"The job I had. I mean, the entire assembly line on that particular product. They took it off the market for some reason; they never explained anything to anybody, but Gloria—she was the girl who worked next to me— Gloria told me they gave everyone notice and shut things down. Several of the women went to work somewhere else in the plant, but those of us who were having babies never went back there to work. We all ended up working for different companies. I guess I wasn't the only one with money troubles, but there really wasn't anything else I could have done. I wanted to stay home and take care of Katie, but I *couldn't*."

"Well, that happens to a lot of people these days," Nathan said. "If the kid can't understand that, there's not much you can do about it. But there must be something more than the fact that she's got odd eyes and doesn't cry that makes sitters uneasy. How did she get along with her grandmother?"

Monica sounded muffled. Maybe she was bending

over, putting the meat in the broiler or something.

"Well, I was never really chummy with Joe's mother. She blamed me for the divorce, though it wasn't any more my fault than his. And even when our marriage was OK, Mother Welker and I weren't buddies. I guess it was just one of those situations where two people don't especially hit it off. So she never talked to me very much. But I think, especially the last couple of years, that Katie made her nervous, too."

"How? What did she do?"

"Nathan, I don't know. She didn't come right out and *say* Katie was strange, she just sort of hinted around. For one thing, I know she thought any kid who read as much as Katie does—and she learned to read when she was only three, all by herself!—was different. But other kids have done that, so it wasn't just that. And she never seemed to have any friends. I talked to one of her teachers, once, and she acted as if Katie were different, too, but I couldn't pin her down. She said there always seemed to be disturbances when Katie was around. I asked what that meant, and she was evasive; but it seems that kids don't like her for some reason. Yes, I was nervous about bringing her to live with me, and not only because of the added expense. I don't know what to do with her!"

This was all very interesting. Katie had eavesdropped on Grandma Welker's conversations sometimes, but all Grandma and her friends talked about were other old ladies and what Pastor Grooten said at prayer meeting and recipes for things like rhubarb crumble.

Katie edged a little closer. It was disturbing to listen to Monica and Nathan talking about her this way, but it was informative, too. She'd never known about her mother working for the Curtis Pharmaceutical Company, or keeping in touch with the women she'd worked with there.

"What was the stuff you handled at the drug company?" Nathan asked now.

"What?"

"The drug you were preparing, or whatever you did. What was it called? What was it used for?"

"It was called Ty-Pan-Oromine. It was a pain killer," Monica said. Katie had moved far enough now so that she could see her mother. Monica turned over the steaks and closed the broiler door on them again.

"They come up with new medications and get rid of the old ones all the time," Monica said. "Isn't there any salad dressing left?"

Nathan rummaged in the refrigerator door. "French style." He put it on the table. "Did you ever take any of the stuff? Ty-Pan-whatever it was?"

"Oh, I guess we all took some once in a while. When we had headaches or something, and one girl took it for cramps. It worked fine."

"It worked, but they stopped making it. Monica, what if they decided to stop making it because it was dangerous?"

"What difference does it make, after all these years? If it was dangerous, it's no longer in use."

"Yeah," Nathan said, looking at her with his arms crossed on his chest. He reached up and scratched his beard. "But what if it had already done some damage to you. I mean, they know now that some drugs are very bad for pregnant women. They can harm the baby, can't they?"

Monica forgot about the dinner. "What are you talking about? That working for Curtis may have done something to *Katie?* What could it do? I mean, she's bright, and she had the usual number of fingers and toes and—"

"And she's strange," Nathan finished for her. "Maybe that's why. Maybe she's a—a mutation, or something. You know, like if she'd had radiation."

For a moment Katie thought Monica was going to be upset, but then she laughed. "You read too much science fiction. If it affected Katie, it would have affected the other women's babies, too, wouldn't it? And they're all right. Someone would know, if there was something serious."

"Are they all right? Have you seen those other kids?" Nathan asked.

"Well, no. But I told you, I keep in touch with several of them. They'd have said if . . ."

Her voice trailed off, and Nathan spoke very quietly. "Would they? Have you told anybody you have a kid with silver eyes who has something very strange about her?"

Right then the timer went off on the stove, and Monica forked the steaks onto a warm platter. "Call Katie, let's eat," was all she said.

It was a heck of a time to end a conversation, Katie thought.

5

D U R I N G the meal Monica and Nathan talked about other things, leaving Katie out of it most of the time. She didn't care. She had a lot to think about all by herself.

Ever since she could remember, she had taken it for granted that she was different from other people. She hadn't wondered why, especially; she'd thought it was just one of those things that happen, like the two-headed calf that had been born on Mr. Tanner's farm once. The calf had died, but Katie hadn't thought her peculiarities were such that *that* would happen to her.

Until now, as far as she was concerned, she was simply a freak of nature. It hadn't occurred to her that something might have happened to *make* her different.

She didn't think she liked Nathan very much. He was too loud and too bossy, and how could you like someone who smelled of tobacco and beer and called you "kid" instead of by your name?

But maybe Nathan had something. About her mother

working in the pharmaceutical plant. About the drug Monica had handled and had taken for a headache. It really might have caused something to go wrong with Katie, who had been growing inside of her.

And if Nathan was right—Katie forgot to eat, engrossed in the idea—that she was the way she was because of the stuff Monica had worked with, what about the babies those other women had had? All about the same time as Katie herself had been born? Was Ty-Pan-Oromine responsible for her silver eyes and this ability to move things by thinking about moving them? And if it was, were those other kids like herself? Somewhere out there in the world, were there more "different" kids, who would be her own kind?

How could she find out?

A trickle of excitement moved like electricity in her veins. Monica had said she still kept in touch with some of the women she had worked with. There had been four of them altogether who got pregnant while they were working together. That meant there coud be three more kids out there who wouldn't think Katie was strange at all.

"Katie? You want a piece of apple pie?"

She came to, cleaned off her plate, and accepted the pie. It wasn't very good, compared to Grandma Welker's pie. Instead of being light and flakey, the crust was tough. And while there were sugar and spices mixed in with the apples, there sure wasn't any butter, and no rich cream to pour over it. Store-bought pies weren't any better than store-bought cookies.

She noticed that Monica and Nathan didn't eat their crusts, either. She wondered if Monica ever baked or cooked anything that took more than fifteen minutes.

That was one thing she was going to miss about Grandma Welker: her cooking.

She expected maybe Monica would assign her the job of doing dishes, but she didn't. (At home in Delaney, Katie had always either washed or wiped the supper dishes.) Here, though, there was a dishwasher, and while Nathan carried his beer and his cigarette into the living room and turned on the TV, Monica quickly rinsed the dishes and stowed them in the dishwasher. After that, she opened up the paper to the babysitter ads and started calling the numbers.

"I've found someone," she said in relief after the fourth call. "A Mrs. Gerrold. She'll be here in the morning at eight. And Katie, I hope for better things from you tomorrow. If there's any difficulty at all, I want to know precisely what it is."

Nathan was watching a ballgame, and Monica sat down beside him on the couch. Katie didn't care about watching baseball any more than she enjoyed playing it. She withdrew to her room and finished *The Scarlet Pimpernel*. Mrs. M. was right; it was a good book. She decided she probably had time to read the western by Louie L'Amour before it was time to turn off the light; it wasn't very long.

And all the time she was reading, somewhere in the back of her mind, Katie was making plans.

Mrs. Gerrold arrived at five minutes to eight, and Monica let her in. She didn't look anything like Mrs. Hornecker, but Katie didn't think she'd like her any better.

Mrs. Gerrold was fat. Grossly, disgustingly fat. She made herself clear at once.

"I don't do no housework," she said. "And I got to catch my bus at exactly five ten. It's the last one runs out to my neighborhood. And I don't walk out to the park with the kids, things like that. I got corns, and my feet hurt too much to walk to the park."

Even without the corns, Katie guessed that the woman's feet would hurt, just from holding up all that weight.

"Yes, well, I have to run," Monica said. "I hope you and Katie get along all right. And if you wouldn't mind putting the meat loaf in the oven about four-thirty, and three baked potatoes. I mean, put in three potatoes to bake."

"I don't cook, neither," Mrs. G. said, shifting a wad of gum from one cheek to the other.

"I can put in the meat loaf," Katie said. She knew Monica had it already mixed, standing in the refrigerator. She wasn't sure what Monica was paying Mrs. G.; but it seemed a waste of any money at all to pay someone to be in the apartment doing nothing just so Katie would have company she didn't want.

Mrs. G. was not a reader. She was a TV addict. She poured herself a cup of coffee and carried it to the living room, settling herself in the biggest chair. She watched a game show, and then the soap operas started. Katie didn't stay around. She only watched *The Edge of Night* or *Search for Tomorrow* or *As the World Turns* when she was too sick to read. But she did keep an interested eye on Mrs. G.

During the commercials, Mrs. G. tottered out to the kitchen for snacks. Watching the diminishing supply of fruit, cookies, and sandwich materials, Katie wondered if there'd be enough food to last out the day. The coffee cup, sitting on the floor beside Mrs. G.'s chair, was joined by banana peels and bread crusts and, finally, a beer can. And in the kitchen the crumbs and stains accumulated. Maybe she wouldn't have to do anything about this one, Katie thought. Monica would get fed up with this slob all by herself.

She didn't waste all her time that morning, though, thinking about the new sitter. She went into Monica's bedroom and began to go through her desk drawers. If she could only find some of the correspondence Monica had had from the women who worked with her at the drug company.

For someone who kept a reasonably tidy apartment, Monica sure had a messy desk. There were all kinds of old bills, cancelled checks, and odds and ends. Monica didn't have any real family—her parents had both died when she was a teenager—and she didn't like the aunt who had reared her, so they only wrote once or twice a year. She had some cousins, and though she'd never talked about them, Katie guessed she wasn't good friends with them, either. There was so much junk that for a while Katie was sure Monica was the kind of person who saved all her letters, but at the end of the top drawer she hadn't found any. She closed that drawer and started on the next one.

Ah, might be something here. There was a photograph album and what looked like keepsakes. Katie laid the album on top of the desk and began to read through it.

There was Monica in a cap and gown, graduating from high school. She was smiling, and very pretty. There were lots of other snapshots of people who didn't look familiar, and then one that did. Katie didn't need the handwritten caption beneath the picture of the dark-haired, laughing young man.

Joe. That was her father. She wondered where he was, and if he even knew yet that Grandma Welker had died. He wasn't much of a one for writing letters, although he usually sent a card for his mother's birthday, and one for Katie's. They were usually late, as if Joe didn't remember until the actual day. And at Christmas he sent a box for them both; Katie still had the teddy bear he'd given her when she was seven. She'd slept with it for almost two years. Last Christmas, though, he'd only sent a card and a check, and told Grandma to buy Katie something.

The "something" had been a new winter coat and a pair of boots, and while she loved the cherry red coat with its matching hood, Katie wished he'd picked out something especially for her, himself, like the teddy bear.

Of course, she was way too old for teddy bears now. She wished she could let him know how much she'd like to have books, but he didn't stay in one place long enough for her to write to him very much. And when she did write, he didn't write back, although sometimes he'd call on the phone. Katie always felt excited when he called, and shy, too; ahead of time, she'd think of what she wanted to say the next time she got the chance, and then when he was talking long distance from Texas or Montana or wherever he was, her mind would go blank. Last time, he'd said to her, "Remember, I love you, baby," and after she'd hung up Katie went out in the back yard with the chickens and avoided everybody for a while. She wasn't sure why that had made her sad, to be told that her father loved her, but it had.

She forgot what she'd come looking for, slowly turning the pages of the album. There were her parents on their wedding day, looking young and skinny and happy. And there was a picture of herself as an infant, chubby and stupid-looking, sitting on a blanket.

Katie found a lot of pictures of herself when she was very small. After she got to be about two years old—she could tell by the number of candles on the cake that the picture was taken on her second birthday—they didn't seem to take so many any longer. Was that because they had lost interest, or because she wasn't cute any more, or what? Maybe by that time they all knew she was peculiar, and so they didn't care about pictures any more.

She leafed onward and saw herself beside a Christmas tree when she was three. It must have been when she was three, because by the time she was four, Katie had been with Grandma Welker.

Katie studied her own small face. She'd looked happy, then. She hadn't found out for sure yet that she was peculiar.

After that there weren't any more pictures of Joe Welker. There were Katie's school pictures, always solemn and sometimes with the light reflecting off her glasses, and she usually looked scared. Never happy.

There were more snapshots of Monica with people Katie didn't know, and Katie almost overlooked the important one because it was just a bunch of young women smiling into a too-bright sun. Nothing was written underneath it, but on impulse Katie slipped it out of the little corner things that held it in the book, and turned it over.

The gang at Curtis—Gloria Haglund, Monica Welker,

Stephanie Donohue, Sandra Casey, Fern Lamont, and Paula VanAllsburg.

Katie turned it back over with more interest, to re-study the snapshot. Gloria, Monica had said, Gloria was one of the women who worked next to her.

She tried to see if any of them had their stomachs bulging out, as if they were pregnant, but the photographer had stood too close to them. He didn't get their stomachs in the picture.

Still, she knew their names now. If only there would be something in Monica's things to indicate where they were, and which of them had had the babies. The babies who would now be almost ten years old, and who might be like herself.

Katie kept on going through the rest of the album, but it didn't have anything interesting in it. Some snapshots of Nathan at the beach, his muscles bulging, and some of Monica in a bikini. Grandma Welker would have made disapproving noises over that one. She thought bathing suits ought to cover up your belly button.

The album had taken enough time so that Katie's breakfast had worn off. She went out to get something to eat, and Mrs. G. didn't even notice. She was eating a Danish that Katie thought was intended for Monica's breakfast tomorrow, her eyes glued to the screen where a man and a woman were having a heated argument.

Mrs. G. had eaten all the bananas except one overripe one. Katie looked at it and decided she didn't want it, either. She made herself a peanut butter sandwich and decided she might as well eat the last orange in the bowl before Mrs. G. got to that.

Back at the desk, she was careful not to get either juice or peanut butter on the things she sorted through.

And this time she had a little luck, or at least she thought it was.

Monica had a box of things like old Christmas cards and valentines and one of the first things that showed up when Katie emptied the box onto the desk was a birth announcement.

She snatched it up eagerly, looking at the date before she read the names. September, ten years ago. The baby had been born seventeen days after Katie's birthday on the tenth.

A girl. Kerrie Louise Lamont, born to Fern and Charles.

Katie was so excited she nearly choked on the peanut butter sandwich. That girl was one of them; and now she, Katie, knew the father's name, too. Was there any chance they still lived here in the city?

She had to go out into the living room to find a phone book. Mrs. G. was chewing away like crazy, and she'd poured herself some more coffee. The cup had left rings on the coffee table, and there were crumbs inside the rings. Mrs. G. had had a peanut butter sandwich, too. She didn't pay any attention to Katie. The quarrel on the screen had ended, and the man and woman were kissing each other passionately.

Katie averted her eyes from both the TV and from the sitter, and opened the phone book. Lamont, Charles Lamont. Lambert, Lambeth, Lamme, Lamon, Lamoreaux —no Lamonts at all.

Disappointment stabbed at her. It had seemed an ordinary name, one that she'd find half a dozen of, anyway, so she'd have to call them all. Of course, the Lamonts could have moved anywhere.

She wondered what Monica would do if she asked

about them. She'd certainly realize that Katie had been listening to her conversation with Nathan, and she probably wouldn't like that. And if she knew Katie had heard it all—that they thought she was strange and they were uncomfortable being around her—it wouldn't exactly be a step toward having a good family relationship. On the other hand, Katie didn't think she could actually come right out and admit to Monica just how different she *was* and ask for her help in finding the other kids who might be like her. And it was possible that those kids had never said anything about what they could do either, especially if their parents were worried and frightened the way Monica was.

She put the phone book aside and stood up. There was a commercial on, and Mrs. G. turned her head away from the screen for a minute. "As long as you're up, bring me the salt shaker, will you?" She had an apple, polishing it against her enormous belly.

Mrs. G. had only been here for a few hours, and already the living room looked like a garbage dump. Katie stared at her in disgust and decided to bring the salt without going after it. It was a fairly heavy shaker, and Katie didn't do too good a job of steering it; it bumped the wall, coming through the doorway, and spilled a little when it landed in Mrs. G.'s lap.

The sitter didn't even notice. Her attention was back on the screen, where a bunch of people in white uniforms were pretending they were doctors and nurses. "Thanks, kid," was all the woman said.

Later Katie wondered if, for just a minute, she hadn't been really crazy. Because she had an impulse to do something to shake the stupid woman out of her eating and TV-watching rut. If she'd known how to make her-

57

self bleed (without hurting) she'd have tried that, just to see if Mrs. G. noticed.

Instead, she created a terrific wind, the best one she'd ever done, and sent things swirling around the living room. The curtains swayed, the newspapers slithered off the coffee table onto the floor, the pages of an open book flipped rapidly. And then, when Katie gritted her teeth and closed her eyes and used the final ounce of power left within her, she swooshed the wind across Mrs. G so that it blew her hair off.

Well, after a few horrified seconds Katie realized it was a wig; the mop of hair fell off and dangled over the arm of the chair. Mrs. G. wasn't bald, she just had thin hair, and the hairpiece was to make it look as if there was more of it.

At least that got her attention. The sitter looked around, clutched at her denuded head, and watched as the *TV Guide* fluttered to a stop on the rug.

"Shut the doors! The wind's blowing everything to pieces!" she yelled. She picked up the wiglet, which looked like some strange little dead creature, and settled it back on her head. "While you're up, switch over to Channel Four, will you?"

Katie gave up. Let Monica deal with her. She went back into the bedroom and began going through more of the things from Monica's box. She was looking for birth announcements, personal letters from any of the people in the picture of the drug company employees, that sort of thing.

By the time she had finished, Katie had found two more announcements of births within a month of her own: Dale John Casey, and Eric Arnold VanAllsburg.

Four of them, all born in September, almost ten years

ago, to women who had worked with the drug that was so dangerous the company had stopped making it.

Katie kept out the three birth announcements and shoved everything else back into the box and replaced it in the desk drawer. A new tremor of excitement ran through her.

Somehow, she thought, she had to find the other three kids and see if they were like *her*.

6

SHE would have gone through the telephone book immediately, looking for the other names, if it hadn't been for the sitter. Mrs. G. had turned down the volume on the TV and was now talking on the telephone. To get the phone book, Katie would have had to approach within inches of her, and she didn't feel like doing that.

"Little skinny kid with glasses," Mrs. G. was saying. She paused and held one hand over the receiver to speak to Katie. "Talking to my sister. Why don't you go outside and play or something." She lifted her hand and continued the conversation. "It's a long way over here on the bus. I don't know if it's worth it, for babysitter money. And I liked to starved, no more'n they keep in the ice box."

Indignant, Katie turned away. Fortunately, she'd just remembered that she had Mrs. M.'s receipt for the paper, and she decided to take it over and see how Lobo was.

Mrs. M. opened the door wearing a muumuu with lavender and white flowers against a deep purple background. "Well, come on in," she said, opening the door wide. "You back for more books already?"

"No. I mean, yes, I read both of them, and they were good, but I forgot to bring them back. I just wanted to get away from that sitter and give you this." She handed over the receipt, then noticed Lobo lying on a red velvet cushion on one end of the couch. "How are you, Lobo?"

It happened again. She *knew*, as certainly as anything. Katie turned to Mrs. M. "He feels better, and he'd like some chopped liver."

Mrs. M. laughed. "Oh, you can talk to cats, eh? Well, maybe you can. He sure had a bladder infection, just like you said. And he ought to be better, taking medicine that cost twelve fifty for a little bitty bottle. All right, lover," she said to the cat, "I'll get your liver."

While she was getting it, she talked to Katie over the top of the refrigerator door. "Why do you need to get away from the sitter?"

"She's a pig," Katie said. She almost added, *she's big and fat*, but decided against it. Mrs. M. was pretty big, too, but she wasn't a pig like Mrs. G. "She's got a whole pile of banana skins and apple cores on the floor beside her chair, and her coffee cup made marks on the table, and all she does is watch TV, except now she's talking to her sister on the phone. Probably long distance, on our bill."

"Sounds like a good one," Mrs. M. agreed. "You like a cookie?"

The cookies were oatmeal and raisin, and homemade. Katie chewed appreciatively. She wondered if Mrs. M. would have any ideas about how to find out where those other kids born in September almost ten years ago had gone.

She knew she was taking a chance. But she had to find those kids. And if Mrs. M. didn't get excited about Katie being able to talk to cats, why, maybe she would understand about the other things, too.

Before she knew it, she was telling Mrs. M. the whole thing. How the other kids didn't like it when she made the ball move away from her face, or whisked back a dropped pencil without touching it, or retrieved her shoe when two boys were tossing it back and forth between them by just mentally pulling it down from above their heads.

Mrs. M. seemed very interested. She poured Katie a glass of milk and made herself some tea, and put a plate of cookies between them on the table.

"It isn't just that I can move things, though," Katie said, reaching for her third cookie. "It's something in my looks, because lots of times I haven't done *anything*, and they just look at me and back away."

"It's your eyes," Mrs. M. said, nodding. "Very different. People don't like people who are different."

"But why not? Having silvery colored eyes doesn't hurt anybody, does it?"

"No, not really. Any more than having one blue eye and one green one does, but the other kids tease Jackson Jones about that. Make stupid remarks. My brother had a birthmark, right here," she touched the side of her face. "It was shaped sort of like an insect, so the kids called him Spider Face. After he got grown up, he had it taken off, but people who've known him a long time still call him Spider."

"You can't have your eyes taken out," Katie said.

"No. I think maybe you can get contact lenses, when

you grow up, though. They can make it seem as if your eyes are a different color, if that's what you want."

"Really? But it'll be a long time before I'm grown up. And even with contact lenses I'll still be different, won't I?"

"Seems to me you're better than most folks. And maybe that's it; they don't want anyone to be better, or smarter, or more powerful in any way. They're afraid of people who are different, so they make fun of them. Attack them. It's foolish, but it's the way people are. What else can you do, besides make things float around in the air?"

Katie shrugged. "Nothing. And that isn't very useful. I mean, it's easy to make the pages of my book turn without touching them, but it doesn't save enough energy so I can use it to do something else really important. And it's easy to bring myself a banana from the kitchen without getting up and going after it, but it would only take a minute to get it the regular way."

Mrs. M. thought about that. "Well, you said it's getting stronger. You can move heavier things now than when you first started. So maybe there'll be a use for it, one of these days."

"But do I have to wait until I'm grown up? And won't I still be a freak? Won't people still be afraid of me and hate me because I'm different? I don't know any grownups who can make things move just by thinking about it."

Mrs. M. nodded her uncombed head. "It's a problem all right. Let's see you move something. Can you put sugar in my tea?"

"I don't know. Sometimes I spill things that aren't in a package or something," Katie warned.

"We can clean it up. Go ahead, put some sugar in my tea," Mrs. M. urged.

So Katie lifted the spoon from the sugar bowl, floated it unsteadily across the table, and dumped it triumphantly into the teacup. She only spilled a little into the saucer.

"Hey, that's very good! I wish I could do that. Seems like it would come in very handy, especially when you get old and stiff, or when you're sick. I can see, though, that it might cause trouble if people see you doing it, when they don't understand it."

"I think my grandma thought I was a witch, or something. It scared her. And I didn't even do very many things in front of *her*."

"Well, maybe all you can do is just be careful. Not do it when anyone's looking."

"Yeah. That's what I do, mostly, now. But maybe, if there are other kids like me, I could find them. It would be nice to know someone else like me."

So she went on and told Mrs. M. about Nathan's theory of how something happened to the women who were pregnant when they worked with the drug that was so dangerous the company stopped making it.

"Do you think that's possible?" Katie asked when she'd finished.

Mrs. M. considered. "Well, I've read about such things. Of course, I thought it was science fiction. But twenty years ago men going to the moon was science fiction, and now they can really do it. And if it happened to you, seems like it could happen to somebody else, too. Not going to the moon, I mean making things move by themselves. So maybe there's a lot of people out there like you. Only they've all been treated like freaks, so they've gone underground. You know, they pretend to be the same as everyone else."

"It's hard work to keep pretending all the time. How am I going to find them, then?" Katie wondered. She brought the three birth announcements out of her pocket and tried to smooth the creases out of them. "I already looked in the phone book for the name of Lamont. There aren't any at all, so I guess these people have moved away."

"What about the other ones?" Mrs. M. had to get out her reading glasses to look at them. "Eric Arnold Van-Allsburg, born to Paula and Richard. Dale John Casey, born to Sandra and Alfred. Kerri Louise Lamont, born to Fern and Charles. Hmmmm."

Katie waited hopefully for Mrs. M. to come up with a brilliant idea. All she said was, "Get the phone book, and we'll look for the other ones."

Though there were no Lamonts, there were eleven VanAllsburgs (though none of them was named Richard) and seventeen Caseys. Two of the Caseys had the first initial A, so they decided to try those first. Neither of them answered.

Mrs. M. looked at the clock. "Well, they must all be still working. You'll have to call in the evening."

"With Monica and Nathan listening?" Katie asked. "How am I going to do that?"

"Well, I guess you'll have to come over here and use my phone," Mrs. M. decided.

"If they had kids," Katie said slowly, "wouldn't somebody be home during the day?"

"Maybe they leave 'em with a sitter. Speaking of sitters, you think that one you had today will be back tomorrow?"

"I don't know. She said it was a long way to come and didn't pay enough. Maybe Monica will fire her." Katie hoped so. "I can do more things to make her quit, but if I do, and Monica and Nathan find out, they might do something to *me*. I don't think they'd be as understanding as you are."

"Oh, I've been around longer. The more you see," Mrs. M. told her, "the more you learn to accept things. I guess we better not eat any more cookies; they'll spoil your supper."

"I suppose. It's almost five, and everybody will be coming home pretty soon. In fact, Mrs. G. has to catch a bus at ten after, so I don't even know if she'll be around until my mother comes home. I think I ought to see if there's any way I can help Jackson Jones collect from Mr. Pollard. He always makes Jackson come back three or four times before he pays him for the paper."

"I'm not surprised. Mr. Pollard hates cats. He kicked poor old Lobo once, and Lobo limped for a week. What are you going to do?" Mrs. M. sounded most interested.

"I don't know. I'll have to wait and see, I guess," Katie told her.

She wandered back to her own apartment, going by way of the deck to see if anyone was swimming. No one was. What was the use of having a swimming pool if nobody went in it?

Mrs. G. had finally turned off the TV and was picking up her garbage to take it to the kitchen. Katie was disappointed; she'd hoped it would still be in the living room when Monica came home, so Mrs. G. would be fired.

"Well, so long, kiddo," Mrs. G. said, after she'd dumped her dirty dishes into the sink and the rinds, cores, and peelings into the garbage can. "I'll see you tomorrow."

It was absurd that Monica should pay the woman to come here and sit and watch TV and eat Monica's groceries all day. She hadn't paid any attention to Katie at all; she hadn't even asked where she'd been, the hour or more she'd spent in the apartment across the hall. What good was she?

Katie stood on the balcony and watched unhappily as Mrs. G. tottered off to the corner to catch her bus. She intended to come back, and what could you do to frighten off somebody who was so absorbed in soap operas that she didn't even notice what went on around her?

All of a sudden she remembered the meat loaf and potatoes she was supposed to have put in the oven. Katie spun and ran to the kitchen, turning on the oven and getting out the meat loaf Monica had made the night before. Usually they baked such things at 350°. Would it cook fast enough if she turned it up to 400°? She stuck the meat loaf in and got out the potatoes. At home Grandma put big (clean) nails through the potatoes, to make them cook faster, but Katie couldn't find any nails in Monica's kitchen. Well, they'd bake at 400°, too, so maybe it would work out right. Maybe she ought to turn the heat up to 500°. She could turn it back down to the right temperature just before Monica got here, and nobody'd ever know the difference.

She went back to her post on the balcony, waiting for people to show up. Somebody did, although she didn't know who he was.

He was about as old as Nathan, she guessed, only she liked his looks better. He didn't have a beard, and he had a nice, friendly face. He parked his car in the lot—in the space for 3-A, which probably didn't matter since Mr. P. didn't have a car—and came toward the front door below her. When he looked up and saw Katie, he waved.

The new man was tall and had sandy hair and blue eyes. Katie was very conscious of eye color, now; she kept hoping she'd find someone who had silvery eyes like her own. Of course the newcomer was much too old to have been exposed to that experimental drug or whatever it was, but maybe that wasn't the only thing that gave people special abilities.

"Hi," he called up to her. "Do you know if there are any furnished apartments available in this building? I'm looking for one."

Katie leaned over the railing. "I don't know. The sign says furnished and unfurnished. My mother rented this one unfurnished a week ago. The manager lives in the basement, if you want to ask him."

"OK. I will." He grinned at her and went on inside. It would be nice, Katie thought, if Mr. Pollard moved out and this man moved in. He didn't look to be the type who would swear at her if he ran into her on the stairs.

She saw Jackson Jones coming on his bicycle, far down the street. A little dog ran after him, yapping and nipping at Jackson's pant leg.

She could communicate with cats. Could she do the same with dogs? From a block away?

She didn't know if she'd have to say it loud enough for the dog to hear it or not, but it was worth a try.

"Stop that," she said aloud. "Jackson's a nice boy. Don't bite him."

Of course, the dog couldn't hear her. But it suddenly stopped running after Jackson and trotted back into its own yard. So she didn't know if she'd communicated or if the dog had simply gotten tired.

That was something most other people couldn't do, either. Talk to dogs and cats. Well, of course, anybody could *talk* to them, but most people didn't get answers back. Not that she'd had an answer from the dog, but he'd done what she said. She wondered what old Dusty would have had to say, if she'd been able to get him to respond? Dusty had been an old dog when she went to live with Grandma Welker, and he'd had to go live with the Tanners when Grandma died. He'd been a nice old dog, even if he didn't talk to her. She missed Dusty.

Katie turned her head and saw that Mr. P. was getting off the bus in the opposite direction. He saw Jackson Jones and broke stride, then continued on more slowly, carrying his jacket because it was so hot.

She'd bet he didn't intend to pay Jackson today, either, if he could help it, Katie thought. Did he keep the boy coming back time and after time for his money just to be hateful? She decided that he was mean enough to do just that.

They met on the edge of the parking lot, just a few yards out from Katie's balcony. She could look down and see Mr. P.'s bald head, the strand of hair gone askew, and the wallet in his hip pocket, too. Katie's fingers curled around the railing. Could she work that wallet out of the tight pocket?

"Could I collect today, sir?" Jackson Jones asked, as politely as if he hadn't tried to collect several times before.

"Gee, I don't think I've got anything smaller than a twenty dollar bill," Mr. P. said. "I'll look and see, but I'm pretty sure I don't."

He seemed surprised when the wallet almost slid out of the pocket into his hand, and then he opened it up to check its contents.

Katie closed her eyes and gritted her teeth, then looked to see how it was working.

The wallet seemed to writhe in Mr. P.'s pudgy fingers, almost as if it were alive. Probably he'd intended only to pretend to peek into the bill compartment, but instead he suddenly found the bills sliding out past his fingers, moving with a will of their own. They eluded his grasp and went sailing off in several different directions.

Mr. P. yelped and grabbed, nearly falling over his own feet. One bill blew right up against Jackson Jones's shirt and stuck there until Jackson put a hand over it. "This one here's a ten, Mr. Pollard," Jackson said. "I can make change for that."

Mr. Pollard, however, wasn't listening. He was pursuing his money. One bill skidded merrily across the sidewalk, defying his efforts to put a foot on it to stop it; another lodged in a tree branch, blending with the leaves. And a third wafted to the feet of the man who had been looking for an apartment, just as he came out the front door.

"Hey, what's going on?" The newcomer picked up the bill, examined it, and then spotted the twin to it in the tree. "Whose money? Yours?" he asked Jackson Jones.

Jackson was busy writing out a receipt. "Well, part of it's mine, to pay for the paper. The rest of it belongs to him." He gestured toward Mr. Pollard, who had finally managed to capture the last of the bills and was cautiously drawing it out from under his foot.

Mr. Pollard was red-faced and perspiring when he came back and accepted Jackson's receipt. He looked up and saw Katie, and his face got even redder. "Funny," he said to no one in particular, "how that kid is always around when things fly in all directions."

"Oh, how's that?" the newcomer asked.

Mr. P. muttered something Katie didn't understand; she didn't think the other man understood it, either.

"My name's Cooper," the man said. "Adam Cooper. I've just rented Apartment 2-C. Are you one of my neighbors?"

"Hal Pollard, 3-A," Mr. Pollard admitted, accepting the bills that Mr. Cooper handed over to him. "Thanks."

"I hope we got it all. What happened, a sudden gust of wind?"

"I guess so. Excuse me, I think I'll take a swim before supper. It must be ninety-five in the shade."

Well, at last someone was going to use the pool. Katie wasn't sure she wanted to share it with nobody but Mr. P., though.

Jackson Jones called, "Thanks, Mr. Pollard," and then looked up at Katie and grinned. "See you later," he said.

Adam Cooper still stood below her. "Hi, again. Listen, are you busy, young lady, or would you help me haul things in tomorrow morning? When I bring my stuff over? I'll pay you."

Katie shrugged. "Sure. Why not. Are you going to swim in the pool?"

"Not tonight. Maybe tomorrow. Why, you need a swimming partner?"

"Somebody besides Mr. Pollard," Katie acknowledged.

"You don't like Mr. Pollard?" Adam Cooper asked.

"I don't think anybody likes Mr. Pollard. He kicks cats and doesn't pay his bills and tells lies and swears at people even when they don't do anything."

"That right? Sounds terrific. Tell you what, after we get my junk carried in tomorrow, we'll go swimming. OK?"

"OK," Katie agreed, and then, after she'd gone back inside the apartment, she wondered uneasily if her mother would agree to that or if the new tenant fell into the category of "strange men" and was therefore to be treated warily.

She had no sooner gotten inside than she smelled the meat loaf and potatoes.

Oh, no! She'd burned up their supper! Katie jerked open the oven door and the smoke poured out into the room just as Monica put her key in the lock.

7

MONICA inspected the charred food. Nathan said, "Who drank my beer?" and Monica looked at the dirty dishes in the sink.

"Mrs. G. wasn't a very good sitter," Katie ventured.

"Did she drink all three beers, or did you have some?" Nathan demanded.

"Grandma Welker said drinking beer was almost as bad for you as smoking," Katie said, "and besides, it tastes terrible."

Monica ran a finger over the dust left in the fruit bowl. "And she ate all the bananas and oranges and apples, too?"

"I think there's a few left in the refrigerator. She ate your Danish, though."

Monica and Nathan looked at each other, and then at the hard and unappetizing food. "Maybe we could cut the bottom off the meatloaf and the rest would be edible," Monica said uncertainly. "I still have stuff left for salad, if the sitter didn't eat that, too."

Katie was afraid Nathan was going to lose his temper, but he didn't. "Why don't you make the salad," he suggested, "and I'll go after pizza. What do you like on yours, Katie?"

It was the first time he'd ever called her anything but "kid." Did that mean he was beginning to accept her, a little?

"Anything but pineapple," she said. "I had pineapple pizza once, but it wasn't as good."

"OK. Pepperoni, Canadian bacon, mushrooms, olives, sauce and plenty of cheese," Nathan decided. "Be back in half an hour."

They seemed to take it for granted that the new sitter had been responsible for cooking the meat loaf and potatoes at 500°, and Katie didn't volunteer the truth. She thought if they hadn't both been a little late coming home, and she hadn't lost track of the time because she was helping Jackson Jones get his money from Mr. P., it might have come out all right, anyway.

Monica began to make the salad. "How did you get along with Mrs. Gerrold?"

Katie shrugged. "All she did was watch television and eat. Oh, and talk to her sister on the phone. She didn't pay any attention to what *I* was doing. I was gone for several hours, and she never even noticed."

"Oh? Where were you for several hours?"

"Just across the hall. Talking to Mrs. Michaelmas. She's nice. She has a cat named Lobo. Lobo means *wolf*," Katie told her. "Hey, I got an idea! Why don't you ask Mrs. M. if she couldn't keep an eye on me, instead of a sitter? It wouldn't cost so much if she didn't have to come over here and stay, and she wouldn't eat all our food and mess up our apartment. Why don't you ask her?"

Monica considered. "You like her?"

"Yes. She has lots of great books to read. She lent me some of them."

"And she likes you?" Why did Monica have to sound so astonished about that?

"Yes. She gave me cookies. She wouldn't do that if she didn't like me, would she?"

"Maybe I'll talk to her," Monica agreed, and Katie's spirits soared.

It was so warm that evening that after they'd let the pizza settle, Monica and Nathan and Katie all went swimming. Mr. P. had been in and was just coming out. Unlike Nathan, who was tanned and muscular, Mr. P. was pale and looked as if he never did anything more strenuous than swear at kids he met on the stairs or trot to avoid paying the paperboy.

He glowered at Katie even now, when she hadn't done a thing except dip one toe in the water.

Nathan didn't seem to notice that Mr. P. was in a bad humor. "Good day for it, eh?"

"It's been a miserable day," Mr. P. asserted. He picked up his belongings from one of the lounge chairs. "I'd advise you not to leave anything lying around here."

"Why? Somebody in the building steals?" Nathan asked.

"I don't know about steals. But I left my shoes and socks here the other day—way back from the edge of the pool—and some joker poured water over them. The shoes were full when I came to get them." He looked right at Katie when he said that, although he couldn't possibly know she was responsible.

"Well, this is the first time any of us has been down here," Monica said, slipping off her sandals. "I'll race you, Katie."

Katie was a fairly good swimmer. The water was cool and soft as silk against her skin. She didn't beat Monica racing to the far end of the pool, but she nearly tied her. For the first time in a good many days, she forgot all the problems in her life and just gave herself over to enjoying herself.

She had dived to the bottom of the pool and then surfaced for air when she suddenly realized there was someone standing on the edge of the pool.

It was the new tenant, Adam Cooper. He wasn't wearing a bathing suit, but he didn't seem to mind that she splashed a little water on him when she came up.

"Hi," he said. "How's the water?"

"Feels great," Nathan said, floating on his back. "You live here, too?"

"I will, tomorrow. I'd asked the little girl to help me haul things in, in the morning. And then it occurred to me that maybe I'd better talk to her folks, first. Make sure it was all right with them. People get ideas, these days, about strange men and little girls. With no elevators in this place, it will save my legs, if somebody can help with the small stuff. I'll pay her, naturally. My name's Cooper, Adam Cooper."

"Nathan Osmond," Nathan said.

"I'm Monica Welker," Monica said. She'd stopped swimming and clung to the side of the pool. "Well, I guess it's all right, Mr. Cooper, if Katie wants to do it. She'll have a sitter keeping an eye on her, of course."

"Of course. Well, good. I'll see you around ten, then, Katie."

"OK," Katie said. Had he come back tonight just to make sure it was all right with her mother? That seemed nice of him, not to want to risk causing any trouble.

Adam Cooper stood there for a few minutes longer, talking to Nathan and Monica, while Katie tried to see how long she could stay underwater. And finally, when she came up, Mr. Cooper was gone.

In the morning, she thought, she'd get out the phone book and try all the possible names and then, if she didn't get any answers, she'd go back to Mrs. M.'s during the evening and try again.

And if none of the people she called turned out to have kids born that same September, Katie didn't know quite what she was going to do next. All she was sure of was that she would never stop looking until she found some of them, the kids who might be like herself.

"Sure," Mrs. Michaelmas said. "I'll keep an eye on Katie. You don't need to pay me anything unless she gets to be a real nuisance." She winked at Katie. "And in exchange, when I go to visit my sister over the weekend, maybe Katie can look after Lobo so I don't have to put him in a kennel. He hates the kennel, and my sister's allergic to cats so I can't take him with me."

That was settled so easily. Now, Katie thought, if only she could solve some of her other problems.

Monica called Mrs. Gerrold and told her she'd mail her a check. Katie didn't hear what Mrs. G. said back, but whatever it was made Monica's face red, so it must not have been very nice.

* * *

77

It felt strange to be all alone in the apartment in the morning, but good. Katie indulged herself in letting things fly around the kitchen, the knives and forks hurtling toward the table, the cereal box tipping itself over the bowl. She had to pour the milk by hand; otherwise, it wobbled so that it spilled too much.

No doubt she'd get better at that as she went along. When she'd finished eating—allowing an orange to peel itself and divide into sections while she watched it—Katie loaded the dishwasher, wiped up the crumbs, and hung up the dishrag, all without leaving her seat at the table.

It was handy, and it was sort of fun. But Katie didn't really see any special value in being able to move things that way. It didn't make up for being so different that nobody wanted to be her friend.

Except Mrs. M., of course. Now, with no sitter around, Katie decided she could make her phone calls from home. She went down the whole list, but only found someone in three places. When she asked for Eric VanAllsburg at one number, and Dale Casey at the other, she was told impatiently by female voices that she had the wrong number, and they hung up before she could even ask if they knew anyone by that name. Well, probably they'd have said if they did, wouldn't they? She didn't cross off those names, though; maybe she'd try again in the evening when there might be someone else at home.

The third time someone answered—A. Casey—a suspicious voice said, "Who's this?"

"My name's Katie Welker," she said politely. "May I speak to Dale?" She hadn't really thought out what she was going to say to those other kids, if she managed to reach them, but as it turned out it didn't matter. The voice on the other end of the wire said, "Dale ain't here now."

Her heartbeat quickened, though. Because there *was* a Dale Casey. Could he be the one she wanted? "Can you tell me when he'll be home?"

"About six, probably. That's when he usually gets off work."

Off work? That had to mean someone more than ten years old. "I think the Dale I'm trying to reach will be ten years old in September," Katie said. She quickly consulted the crumpled birth announcement. "September the sixteenth."

"I wish you kids would stay off the phone and quit bugging me," the voice said, and the receiver was replaced hard enough so that Katie rubbed at her ear.

Well, she thought, tonight she'd go over and visit with Mrs. M., and they'd call the numbers from her phone. Maybe *then* there'd be more answers. She ought to figure out what she was going to say, too, if she got hold of someone who might be the right one.

Are your eyes silver? Do people back away from you? Are you like me, with no friends because everybody thinks you're peculiar? Can you move things without touching them?

She went downstairs to get the mail, after she saw the postman leaving, and leafed through the envelopes with her mother's name on them. An electric bill, a bank statement—and a letter with a name and return address that made Katie stop dead-still in the middle of the foyer.

Lamont, it said. And the address was in Millersville.

Katie had never been in Millersville, but she'd heard of it. She wondered if there was a map anywhere in the apartment, so she could see how far away it was. It had to be the same Lamont, didn't it, as the one Monica had worked with at the pharmaceutical company?

Katie stared at the magical return address. Fern Lamont was the mother of Kerri Louise; and now that Katie knew where one of the children was, she could hardly wait to find out all about her. How to do it, though? If she simply wrote to her at the address on the envelope and asked outright if Kerri had powers no one else seemed to have, what would happen?

If Kerri *did* have unusual abilities, maybe she'd write by return mail and say so. However, probably she, like Katie, realized that some things were better kept secret, and she might not want to admit anything. And there was also the possibility that anything either of them wrote would be intercepted by some adult who would be more alarmed than amused by any claim to an ability not shared by everyone else. Grownups seemed to think that kids didn't need any privacy, nor deserve any.

If only she could travel to Millersville and see this Kerri in person. Then she would know, Katie thought.

"Hi. You waiting for me?"

Katie turned to see the smiling Adam Cooper coming through the front door. "I was getting the mail," Katie said. "Are you moving in now?"

"Moving in now," Mr. Cooper agreed. "I'll go up and unlock the place while you get rid of your mail, and then you can help me carry my junk, OK?"

It seemed as good a way to pass the time as any. Katie took a moment to copy down the address from Mrs. Lamont's letter, just in case she never saw it again, and then went out to Mr. Cooper's car. It had a lot of odds and ends in it, and Katie helped carry in paper bags and cardboard boxes, and even some groceries. When they were through, though, she looked around the apartment and it didn't look as if anyone had moved in.

"You don't have much stuff," she commented.

"Oh, some of my things are in storage. If I decide to stay here, I'll get them out then. My books, things like that."

Katie hadn't seen any books in the containers they'd carried in. Her interest quickened. "Mrs. Michaelmas lends me books to read."

"Who's that?"

"The lady in 2-B. I don't have to have a sitter any more; Mrs. M. keeps an eye on me."

"She's a reader, eh? And you are, too?"

"Yes."

"Well, I'll let you know when I get my books, and you can see if there's anything you want from the Cooper lending library. What do you say we meet at the pool in ten minutes and take a dip before lunch?"

That sounded all right, so Katie went to change into her suit. She also checked in with Mrs. M. and Lobo. Lobo purred when she ran her hand over his head. He might look evil, but he wasn't; it was only the way his fur was marked. Just like herself, Katie thought. People were scared off because she didn't seem or look the way they thought she ought to.

"You look all better," Katie told the big cat. "You don't hurt any more, do you?"

No. But all she gave me to eat today was dry cat food. I don't like it very much.

Mrs. Michaelmas was watching with interest. "What's he say?"

"He doesn't like dry cat food very much." Why was it, Katie wondered, that Mrs. M. could accept her for what she was, but nobody else could?

Mrs. M. laughed. "I'm not surprised. But it's a lot cheaper than the canned stuff, or tuna or chopped liver. Tell him he'll get something better for supper."

That's nice, Lobo thought. He closed his eyes and stretched out in the sun that came through the windows.

"I don't have to tell him; he understands what you say," Katie informed Mrs. M.

"Oh. Well, I thought he did. Only he never answers me back. Can you do that with all animals? Or just cats?"

"I don't know," Katie admitted. "Lobo was the first one. And maybe a dog down the street understood me yesterday, I'm not sure. He didn't say anything back, though. I don't know what good it does, being able to know what animals are thinking. I can't even tell anyone, or they'll think I'm crazy."

"*I* don't think you're crazy," Mrs. M. said. She stuck a pin in her untidy white hair to keep a strand from falling over her face. "You could be a veterinarian, you know. Be very handy, if you were the doctor taking care of the animals; they could tell you where they hurt and so on."

"I guess it would. I'll have to think about that. It would be more use, though, if I could know what *people* were thinking, instead of animals."

Mrs. M. shook her head, and the pin came out so that the hair fell over her eyes again. "I think you'll be better off if you stick to animals. Could cause all sorts of problems, if you could eavesdrop on people's private thoughts.

I don't think you'd want to, once you found out what they were like. You're not going swimming alone, are you?"

Katie ran a hand over her new bathing suit, the one Monica had bought for her after learning that there was a private pool at the new apartment house. "No. Monica won't let me go in alone. She says it isn't safe, even if you're a good swimmer. I helped Mr. Cooper move into 2-C and now we're going to swim. Why don't you come with us?"

"Me? Honey, they don't make bathing suits for fat old ladies like me! On the other hand, there's no law says I can't dangle my feet in the water, is there? Maybe I'll come along and join you."

So Mrs. M. sat on the edge of the pool with her muumuu pulled up to expose pale and surprisingly skinny legs with blue veins in them, while Katie showed off how she could swim and dive. Mrs. M. didn't even care if Katie splashed on her a little; she said it cooled her off.

Adam Cooper swam for a while and then sat beside Mrs. M., talking. He looked good in a bathing suit, Katie thought, almost as many muscles as Nathan, although he wasn't quite as tanned. His sandy hair got lighter as it dried, and he talked easily, pleasantly. She'd bet he'd pay his bills on time, not like Mr. P.

They left the pool when it was lunchtime. Katie wondered if Mr. C. didn't have a job to go to, but he said he was on vacation for a few weeks and didn't have to worry about that right now. He intended, he said, to relax and spend a lot of time around the pool, improving his tan. Nothing like a good tan, he said, to impress the females.

"I'll play lifeguard if you want to swim during the day," he told Katie. "If it's OK with your mother and dad."

"Nathan's not my dad," Katie said quickly. "He doesn't even live with us. He's just a friend of my mom's."

"Oh. Yeah, that's right, he said his name, and it's not the same as yours and your mother's, is it? Are they engaged or anything?"

"I hope not," Katie said, and then wondered if she should have said that.

They were walking toward the stairs that led up to the second floor deck, leaving footprints on the cement.

"Why? Don't you like him?" Adam Cooper asked.

"It's more that I don't think he likes *me*," Katie said.

"Oh? Does he treat you badly?"

Katie shrugged. "Mostly he calls me *kid*, as if I didn't have a name. And he thinks I'm . . ."

She stopped, appalled at what she'd almost said. No sense in giving Mr. C. any reason to think she was peculiar, if he didn't already think so.

"He thinks you're what?"

Her feet had dried off now, and the boards of the stairs were hot. "Oh," she said, trying to sound careless, "I don't think he's used to kids, is all."

"Well," Mr. C. said, "your mother is a very pretty lady. I just wondered if her friend would be upset if I talked to her. You know, around the pool in the evening. I'll probably swim again this evening. Maybe I'll see you then."

That sounded all right to Katie. She wondered if Monica thought Mr. C. was attractive. Katie liked him better than Nathan. For one thing, he didn't smoke: you could always tell; a person stunk of tobacco even when he wasn't actually smoking. And Mr. C. talked to her as if she were a person, not a *kid*.

Mrs. M. came padding along behind them, the wet hem of her muumuu flapping against her shins in a glory of multicolored flowers on a hot pink background. "Seems like a nice fellow," she said, after Mr. C. had turned in at his own door. "I think he likes you, Katie. He kept talking about you, asking questions."

"Oh? What kind of questions?" A little alarm bell rang somewhere in the back of Katie's mind, although she wasn't sure why. Mr. Cooper had no reason to think there was anything wrong with her, did he? She hadn't done anything peculiar while he was around.

It was only, she thought, that she liked him, that it would be nice to have another friend, like Mrs. M. He might not be a friend if he thought she was peculiar.

"Asked me how we got along, you and me, things like that. How much had I seen of you. Why did the baby-sitters both leave."

Katie tried to remember. Had she talked to Mr. C. about the sitters? Only to say that she didn't have one, that Mrs. M. was keeping an eye on her.

She said so long to Mrs. M. and went on into her own apartment, but continued to feel uneasy all the rest of the day.

8

THAT EVENING, when Monica and Nathan again decided to swim, Katie told them she'd be along in a few minutes. As soon as she was sure they'd actually gone down to the pool level, she got out her list of telephone numbers and began to call.

This time she got someone at almost every number, but most of the people who answered didn't know anyone by the names of the kids she gave them. Once when she asked for Eric VanAllsburg, the voice on the other end said, "Just a minute." Then Katie began to tingle all over, anticipating that it would be the right one.

The male voice that answered a moment later, however, sounded a lot older than ten. "Who's this?" he wanted to know.

"Is this Eric VanAllsburg?" Katie asked carefully. Her heart had begun to pound in her chest.

"Eric? This is Harry," the voice said. "Who do you want?"

"I want Eric VanAllsburg."

"My dad must have thought you said Harry. There's no Eric here," the voice said, and the connection was broken.

Katie was disappointed, and she also realized that she didn't really have a plan for starting to speak to the right people when she found them. It would be so much better to meet them face to face, so they could tell she was one of them, too (assuming that the other three were actually all like herself); but she didn't know how to manage that.

And then, under one of the Casey listings, she asked for Dale and heard a woman's voice call, "Dale! Telephone!" and Katie crossed her fingers as hard as she could.

"Hello?"

"Hello, Dale Casey?"

"Yes. Who's this?"

"My name is Katie Welker," Katie said, her mouth dry. "I'm trying to find a Dale Casey who was born September—" she quickly consulted the card from her pocket, "September sixteenth, who'll be ten years old this fall."

There was a long silence. Then the boy on the line spoke cautiously. "Who are you? What do you want?"

It was one of them, Katie thought, with a prickling along her spine. She was *sure* it was.

"Did your mother used to work for the Curtis Pharmaceutical Company, before you were born?"

There was another long silence. "Who did you say you are?"

"Katie Welker. I need to talk to you, if your birthday is September sixteenth, and your mother's name is Sandra."

There was the sound of breathing, nothing else. In

the background she heard a man's voice. "I'm waiting for a call, Dale. Don't tie up the phone."

"Can I call you back?" Katie asked quickly. "Later tonight? Or tomorrow?"

"Tomorrow," the boy said. "OK, tomorrow."

And then that connection, too, was broken. Katie's hand was damp with sweat when she hung up on her end. It had to be the right one, it *had* to be!

She didn't bother to call the rest of the Caseys. And the VanAllsburgs brought no results until the final one.

"Eric? Who you trying to get, Paula's boy?"

Again excitement surged through her. "Yes, that's right."

The woman apparently turned away from the phone to speak to someone else. "Some kid wants to speak to Paula's boy. What's her name, now?"

The reply was unintelligible. The woman came back to Katie. "Paula divorced my brother-in-law and she's remarried now, but we can't remember what her new name is. Something sort of ordinary sounding—Dunlap, or Duncan, or Dugan—something like that."

"Don't you have her number?" Katie asked desperately, picturing the long lists of Dunlaps and Duncans and Dugans in the phone book.

"No. Haven't talked to her since the divorce. Sorry I can't help you." Click. Katie was alone on the line.

Divorced, and remarried, with a different name. That hadn't even occurred to her. How could she possibly trace anyone under those circumstances?

Still, she wasn't totally discouraged this time. Because there was Dale Casey, and she would call him tomorrow.

Katie descended the outdoor stairs to find that Nathan

was swimming vigorously back and forth across the deep end of the pool, and Monica was in a lounge chair talking to Adam Cooper. They didn't see her coming, and Katie's bare feet made no sound on the concrete around the pool.

"So you haven't really seen very much of her until she came to live with you just a few days ago, then," Mr. C. was saying, and Monica fluffed up her short blonde hair and replied, "No, not since she was less than four years old."

They were talking about her. He'd asked questions of Mrs. M., and now of her mother. Why? Why should a grown man be so inquisitive about a little girl?

Adam Cooper had an easy way of speaking, relaxed and friendly. "Must be quite a change in your life, to have a ten-year-old after not having a child around in such a long time."

How did he know she was ten, or almost ten? She was small, and most people took her for younger than she was. Had Monica told him her age?

Katie stood still, a few yards behind them, and once more the uneasiness rose within her.

"I guess you had trouble with sitters for her? Didn't get along with her or something?"

The chill crept through Katie, although it was still hot. Why was he asking questions about her?

She remembered a time, last year, when a substitute teacher had sent her to the office for creating a disturbance. It hadn't been Katie's fault, at all; at least, *she* didn't think so. The boy behind her had been poking her in the back with something hard and rather sharp, and saying nasty things to her, trying to get her to turn around. The substitute, whose name was Miss Cottrell, had spoken very sharply to the class about the need for absolute silence while they did their spelling test. "I will not tolerate any talking at all," she had said in a voice that promised severe retaliation if they disobeyed.

Of course, that only made the kids outrageous. They always tried to take advantage of substitutes, doing things they would never have tried with Mrs. Anderson. Two boys tossed erasers across the room the second Miss Cottrell turned to write on the board, and one of them hit her in the back of the head and left white chalk dust on her dark hair. And Jimmy Polchek stuck out his foot and tripped Charlie Foster so that instead of walking up to sharpen a pencil, Charlie fell into the wastebasket.

And then Derward English started poking Katie in the back even harder. She was good at spelling and was trying to listen to the words and get them all spelled correctly and written in her best penmanship. She was good at that, too.

Only it was hard with Derward pestering her. He was always pestering someone. Once he'd locked some girls in an outhouse when they were on a class picnic at a park, and it had been over an hour before anyone heard them yelling and let them out. Derward had been suspended for three days because of that. Not that Derward minded; he had returned to school boasting that his father had taken him fishing for three days.

When Katie talked about it at home, Grandma Welker said scornfully that people as stupid as Derward's father contributed to the delinquency of minors.

"Anybody in this house who misbehaves in school won't get a three-day fishing trip," Grandma said with a cross glance at Katie. "She'll get three days locked up in her room on bread and water."

Katie didn't think Grandma would really have kept her on bread and water, but she wasn't sure enough of it to take any chances.

She'd tried to ignore Derward, but after a few minutes of feeling the point of his pocketknife jabbing more and more painfully between her shoulder blades, Katie had used all the force she could muster and turned the thing back away from herself.

The next thing she knew, Derward was yelling, and there was blood all over his hand and his desk, and when Miss Cottrell came to the back of the room, she was very angry.

"What happened?" she wanted to know.

And Derward, rat that he was, had blamed it all on her.

"Katie did it, she made me get stabbed, she practically rammed the knife into my hand! She did it on purpose!"

So Derward had been sent to the nurse, who decided that since he'd had a recent tetanus shot, it wasn't serious enough for more than a Band-Aid, and Katie was sent to the office.

Katie remembered standing in front of the principal's desk, her legs quivering, and being asked for her version of the story.

What could she say? That she'd used some mental force that nobody else seemed to have to twist the knife against the boy who was jabbing her with it?

"It was *his* knife," Katie said. "He was fooling around with it, poking me."

"And so you twisted around and cut him with it?" the principal asked.

"I jerked away," Katie said, "and somehow he cut himself. I can still feel where he poked me."

The principal looked at the back of her blouse, but he said there was no cut in it. "Do you want the nurse to look at your back and see if there is a mark on your skin?"

"No," Katie said. If there was no tear in her shirt, it was unlikely that there'd be a mark on her skin. "But it was his own fault."

In the end, nothing happened to either of them, Katie or Derward. They were sent back to class, where spelling was all over and the kids were doing arithmetic. But all the kids looked at Katie out of the corners of their eyes.

Katie still remembered the way the principal and the teacher had looked at her. Not at Derward, but at *her*.

And Monica was now telling Adam Cooper all about the trouble with the sitters. Katie stood quite still and listened to what a blabbermouth her mother was, saying how Mrs. H. had found Katie "too difficult" to deal with, although she'd been unwilling to say specifically why, and Mrs. G. had been unsatisfactory, too.

"The first one, what was her name? Hornecker? She was all right, except that she didn't get along with Katie? I wonder if you still have her phone number," Mr. C. said. "I have some friends who are looking for a sitter, and their little boy is only two. Maybe she'd do better with a young child."

"Why, yes, I guess I still have it. Or it's probably in the paper; that's where I got both their numbers, in the newspaper," Monica said. She turned her head then, and saw Katie. "Well, hi, we thought you'd changed your mind about swimming."

She almost had, Katie thought. She looked at Mr. C.

and he was grinning, friendly, but she didn't believe for a minute that he wanted to ask Mrs. H. about sitting for his friends' little boy. He'd been asking questions of Mrs. M. about her, and now he was pumping Monica. Katie didn't know why, but it made her afraid.

"I'll race you to the other end of the pool," Adam Cooper offered, but Katie shook her head.

"I don't feel like racing," she said. "I don't feel like swimming, even. I think I'll go see Mrs. M."

She turned and went back up the wooden steps and along the deck to Mrs. M.'s patio doors, which were open to catch a little breeze. She looked back down and saw that Mr. C. was watching her, and Monica was leaning toward him, saying something.

"Come on in," Mrs. M. called out. She was sitting with her feet in a dishpan of water. "Excuse me, but my feet swell up in this weather. There's a pitcher of iced tea in the icebox; why don't you get us each a glass of it?"

Katie did so, adding sugar to both of them; it was the only way she could stand the taste of the tea.

"My grandma used to call it an icebox, too, just like you do," she observed, settling onto the sofa beside Lobo, who opened one eye briefly and then went back to sleep.

"Oh, I guess all us old-timers got used to saying icebox," Mrs. M. told her. "They didn't have refrigerators when I was a girl. A man came around twice a week with blocks of ice, and we had a sign we put in the window to show how many pounds we wanted. You don't look like you got wet."

"I didn't." Katie sipped at the tea. "They're talking about me, Mr. C. and my mother."

"Oh? Well, we all talk about the people we like," Mrs. M. said, wriggling her toes in the water.

"I don't think it's because they like me," Katie said. "He's asking more questions about me."

"That doesn't mean he doesn't like you, does it?"

"Did you tell him how old I am?" Katie asked.

"No. I don't think you ever said how old you are. Nine? Eight and a half?" Mrs. M. guessed.

"I'll be ten in September."

"Oh, excuse me. I didn't mean to be insulting. I should have known; anyone who reads adult books the way you do would have to be close to ten. Come to think of it, maybe you did tell me you were ten. I forget things these days."

"Everybody guesses me younger, because I'm not very big," Katie said.

After a while, when she went home, she asked Monica if she'd told Mr. C. how old she was.

"What?" Monica said. She was somewhat distracted; it sounded as if she and Nathan had been quarreling on their way up from the pool.

"My age," Katie said patiently. "Did you tell him I was ten?"

"No, I don't think so. Nathan, aren't you going to stay and watch the news?"

"No," Nathan said. "I'm surprised you even noticed whether I was here or not, the way you spent all evening talking to that jerk."

"He isn't a jerk. He's just a nice man who doesn't know anyone here," Monica said.

"So why doesn't he go meet someone else? Why you?"

Katie could see they were building up to a real fight. She dimly remembered that her mother and her father had sometimes argued, when she was little; she didn't want to listen, and she went into her own room.

94

She wasn't really thinking much about Monica and Nathan, though. She was wondering how Adam Cooper had known how old she was and wondering, too, why it seemed so important to her to know how he'd learned that she was nearly ten.

9

AS SOON as Monica had gone to work in the morning
—with a headache, she said, and Katie wondered if it
was because she and Nathan had had a real fight before
he left the previous night—Katie called the number
where she'd reached Dale Casey.

A man's voice answered, a gruff voice.

"May I speak to Dale, please?"

"He's busy now," the man said. "He's got chores to
do before he can talk to anybody. He's got to weed the
garden and mow the grass."

Katie thought quickly. "Couldn't—couldn't he call me
back? Couldn't I leave my number?"

"Well, I guess so. What is it?"

She told him the number, and repeated her name,
hoping the man was writing it down. But though she
waited in the apartment all morning, no one called.

While she was waiting, she sat down and composed a
letter to the girl, Kerri Lamont, and addressed it to the
return address on the letter Monica had gotten yester-

day from her friend Fern. And then, remembering, she went looking for the letter itself.

Monica hadn't answered it yet, so it was still lying on her desk in the bedroom. Ordinarily Katie wouldn't have thought it very nice to read someone else's mail, but surely this was a special case. Maybe Fern Lamont would say something about Kerri that would give her a clue to what she wanted to know.

The letter was written in terrible handwriting. Mrs. Anderson would have given Mrs. Lamont an F in penmanship, Katie thought. And most of what she wrote wasn't very interesting, all about Mrs. Lamont going back to work now because the kids were in school, except that now they were out for vacation, and she couldn't find a decent sitter, and she didn't really like the job all that much, and Charles (that was her husband) didn't think about anything but bowling and left everything else to her.

Mrs. Lamont sounded like a whiney sort of woman. Katie wasn't surprised that her husband wanted to bowl rather than sit around home and listen to her. She complained about everything. But, finally, at the very end of the letter, Katie found what she'd been looking for.

"The boys run me ragged with their noise and their dirt, but it's still Kerri who bothers me the most. She is such a *strange* child," the word *strange* was underlined, "and I've never been able to talk to her. She just looks at me with those unusual eyes and doesn't say anything back. She doesn't cause trouble, exactly, but she makes everyone uncomfortable, for some reason. I guess I shouldn't say that, she is my own daughter, but it isn't just *me*. Charlie is always looking and raising his eyebrows and asking what's the matter with her. As if I know! Why do men think the kids are a woman's responsibility? He never takes the kids anywhere, or does anything for them except pay their bills—"

There was more, but that was the important part. Kerry had "unusual" eyes, and she was "strange," and her mother didn't understand her, either.

Just like me, Katie thought.

She composed the letter very carefully. Just in case Mrs. Lamont opened it and read it first.

"Dear Kerri:

You don't know me, but I think maybe we could be friends, or at least pen pals. I was born September tenth, the same year as you, and I think maybe we have something in common."

Katie chewed on the end of her pen for a minute, wondering if she should specify anything, and decided not to.

"I like to read, and I like animals," she wrote then. "And I'd sure like to hear from you."

It wasn't much of a letter, but she didn't know what else to put in that wouldn't be dangerous.

Dangerous. Dangerous was walking off the curb without looking to see if there was a bus coming, or being careless with matches, or something like that, wasn't it? Dangerous was a frightening word, and she was surprised, at first, that she'd thought it.

And then she wasn't surprised, because it was the way she was feeling. Afraid, as if something dangerous was happening. If people didn't like people who were different, would they do something about it? Would they be more than just mean, in the way they treated the ones who weren't the same as themselves?

She remembered a boy who'd been in her third grade

class, a black boy named Efram. He'd never done or said a single thing, as far as Katie knew, to make anyone dislike him. Yet some of the kids never wanted him on their team when they played games, although he was as good a player as anyone else. And some of the kids made remarks where Efram could hear them, about his color. She'd hoped, when Efram moved away after a few months, that in his new home he lived close to some other black kids, because he must have been very lonely.

Efram couldn't help it if his skin was a different color, and she couldn't help the way she was, either. She didn't even want to be able to make things fly through the air; what good did it do her?

She found a stamp in a little box on Monica's desk and took the letter to Kerri downstairs for the mailman, try-ing to think how *she'd* react if she got one like it.

Dale Casey still hadn't called back. She'd run up and down the stairs and left the front door open so she'd hear the phone if it rang while she was doing that. She wondered if his father had given him her message. There was also the possibility that Dale wasn't interested in talking to her, though he hadn't sounded that way.

Katie left the door open again and crossed the hall to knock on Mrs. M.'s door. She had Dale's address written down.

"Good morning," Mrs. M. said. Her hair looked like something a bird might choose to make a nest in. "Or is it afternoon? I overslept. That's what I get for staying up half the night to watch the Late Late Show."

She led the way inside and laughed at Lobo, who was stretched full-length across the flowered sofa. "I guess Lobo stayed up all night, too. I think he has a lady friend."

99

Katie brushed a hand over his head. "Have you, Lobo?" she asked.

Lobo opened one eye. *There's a lovely white Persian who lives in the next block.*

"You're right," Katie told Mrs. M. "It's a white Persian."

"Oh, I've seen her. Has good taste, old Lobo has. What's that you've got?" Mrs. M. waggled her fingers at the slip of paper Katie carried.

"An address. I don't know my way around at all. Do you know where it is?"

Mrs. M. had to get her reading glasses in order to see it. Then she got out a city map and her finger pointed out the place to Katie. "Should be right about there."

"And where are we?"

Mrs. M. showed her.

"It doesn't look so far. Do you think I could walk it?"

"You could. The bus runs right there, though, along that red line. Be easier to take the bus. You could get off here and only have two blocks left to walk."

"How about Millersville? Do you know where that is?"

"About ten miles south of here, I think. Wait a minute, and I'll get a state map."

Again Mrs. M. pointed out the place she wanted. Katie wondered if she had enough money in her owl bank to pay for a bus ticket to Millersville, in case Kerri didn't answer. Or in case Kerri *did* answer, and that was the only way to get to see her.

"You're not thinking about taking any trips without telling your ma, are you?" Mrs. M. asked.

"No," Katie said slowly. She wondered if she could get to Millersville and back between the time Monica left in the morning and the time she came home at night. She was pretty sure Monica wouldn't let her go alone, if she asked. "Not right now, anyway," she added, so as to be truthful with Mrs. M.

Across the hall, the telephone rang.

Katie ran, but whoever it was had hung up by the time she got there. She stared in frustration at the phone. Had it been Dale Casey?

She had his number, written on a crumpled piece of paper in her pocket. Katie's fingers were unsteady as she dialed the number, wondering if Mr. Casey would be angry that she'd called twice instead of waiting for Dale to call her back.

But Mr. Casey wasn't angry. No one answered at all, although she let it ring for a long, long time.

That afternoon Katie met Mr. C. in the corridor, carrying a box of books. She knew it was books because it was obviously heavy and there were brightly colored jackets sticking out over the top of it.

"Hi. Open the door for me, will you, and then I won't have to put these down."

Obediently, Katie opened the door to 2-C. The apartment inside was just as she'd last seen it except that there was a coffee mug sitting on the table she could see through the kitchen door. Mr. C. didn't do anything to make his place look lived-in.

Katie didn't have any great amount of experience with men—her father had gone away when she was small, and her grandfather had died so long ago she didn't remember him at all—but she thought most men had a tendency to scatter their belongings around. Nathan, who didn't even live there, left things all over Monica's apartment.

Mr. C. lowered the box to the floor and stood up, dusting off his hands. "Some of these have been in storage for a while and they're dusty. Be a good girl and wipe them off for me, will you? I have another box to bring up."

He was gone, leaving her there with his books. Naturally, Katie couldn't help taking a look at them. She'd never been able to resist a book; and when Grandma Welker didn't approve of her, that had been her punishment—to stay in her room without a book. Katie used to keep one or two hidden, in reserve, just in case.

There were some hardcover mysteries with gory covers, and a lot of paperbacks. Katie looked around for something to use to get the dust off them and settled for a paper towel. The kitchen was so sterile-looking she couldn't believe he'd cooked anything in it. Nathan left crumbs everywhere when he went into the kitchen. There was no toaster, no electric frying pan, no can opener, none of the things Monica had in sight on her counter.

Katie knew it wasn't really polite to poke around in other people's refrigerators, but her uneasy feeling was growing, and she felt compelled to open the door.

There was almost nothing in there. A carton of yogurt, four apples, a quart of milk and another of orange juice. That was all. Nothing to cook.

Suspicion led Katie onward, the paper towel forgotten in her hand. And she was right. There weren't even any pots and pans to cook in, and only plastic utensils to eat with, and paper plates. In the almost-empty cupboard there was a loaf of bread and a jar of peanut butter.

What did it mean? Adam Cooper was more camping out than he was living here.

She heard his feet on the stairs and turned quickly back to the box of books. Her heart was beating fast and loud; it felt like a small frightened animal in her chest.

Mr. C. put down a second box of books beside the first one. "There. Maybe these will make the place feel more like home." He grinned at her, but somehow Katie didn't feel like grinning back.

"That book on top must be one my sister's kids left, the last time they came to visit," Mr. C. said. "Why don't you take it and read it, if you want to? And you can always come back and borrow anything else you want. Do you think these will all fit in that little bookcase?"

Katie stared at the book he'd handed her. *The Headless Cupid*. Well, it did look interesting, though she thought it might be intended for little kids. She'd take it along, what the heck.

"Well," Mr. C. said. "I worked up a sweat, carrying that stuff up here. I think now I'm ready for a swim. What about you?"

When Katie hesitated, he added, "Maybe your friend, Mrs. Michaelmas, would like to come and dangle her feet in the water again. Why don't you ask her?"

Katie *did* want to go into the water, and Mrs. M. was willing to sit on the edge of the pool—today she was wearing a pink and white and lilac muumuu that spread out around her like a gigantic flowered tent—so Katie pushed aside her doubts about Mr. C.

At first it was all right; she and Mr. C. swam vigorously, and the water was cool and refreshing. But then Mr. C. said he had to rest awhile and he went to sit on the edge of the pool beside Mrs. M. To begin with, Katie didn't pay any attention to what they were talking about. And then she heard Mr. C. say, "Has she ever done anything odd when she was with you, Mrs. Michaelmas?"

Katie had been on the bottom and had just bobbed to the surface close to the edge of the pool. She was hidden from the speakers by a bonsai tree in a planter box, and she held her breath—but not to dive back under the water. Was he asking questions about *her* again?

Apparently Mrs. M. thought he was pretty nosey, too. She sounded a bit cross, and Katie could see her blue veined feet as she splashed them impatiently in the water.

"What do you mean by odd?" Mrs. M. asked. "People think I'm odd because I talk to my cat. People think my friend Mr. Upton is odd because all he can talk about is his coin collection. And Mrs. Shaver, upstairs in 3-C, is a vegetarian. Won't even eat butter from cows or eggs from chickens, she's such a vegetarian. What's odd, Mr. Cooper?"

"Hey, I'm sorry! I didn't mean to upset you," Mr. C. said easily. Katie could see his legs, too, tanned and hairy. "I just couldn't help being curious, is all. I mean, Mr. Pollard thinks Katie is able to . . . do things."

"Do things?" Mrs. M. echoed. "Can't everybody do things?"

"Different from what the rest of us can do, he says. Like, Katie's around when a sudden wind blows a door shut in his face and gives him a nose bleed. And the wind also blew the money right out of his wallet and up in the trees and down the street."

"Winds've been blowing for hundreds of years," Mrs. M. said. She reached out a hand to scratch at her shin. "I expect they'll keep on, long after all of us are gone."

"Sure. Only some winds are different from regular ones, don't you think? Winds that happen inside a building, for instance, when Mr. Pollard's briefcase came open and his papers went sailing all over the place."

"Mr. Pollard's a . . . a . . . what's the word the kids use? A jerk? Or do they have a different word for it now? Doesn't matter. He's one of those people who blame their problems on other people. Can't abide the man. Where's that child got to?"

"She's underwater. Katie's a good swimmer," Mr. C. said, and Katie quickly went under and swam out across the pool so that they could see her red bathing suit beneath the surface.

She came up on the far side, gasping for breath, and turned to find them both watching her.

Why did Mr. C. keep asking questions about her? Was he trying to get Mrs. M. to admit that Katie could do things other people couldn't, for some terrible reason?

She didn't know why, but she was convinced that the reason *was* terrible.

Katie clung there, at the side of the pool, a conviction growing deep inside of her. The conviction that Mr. C. had moved into The Cedars Apartments for one reason: to ask questions about Katie, herself. He didn't intend to stay long, only until he'd learned whatever it was he hoped to learn, and that was why he didn't have any pans to cook in and hadn't filled up his refrigerator; and that was why he'd brought some boxes of books, after he found out Katie liked to read. He was going to tempt her with the books and use them to get her to talk to him, and then what?

If he became certain that Katie could make winds blow and other things happen, what was he going to do about it?

10

THE HEADLESS CUPID was a very good book, but Katie couldn't concentrate on it and worry at the same time. So she finally put it aside and stood up.

Monica had come home with a sick headache and hadn't wanted any supper; she was lying down in her room, a cold cloth over her eyes. Katie had had a Mexican TV dinner and had made her own salad to go with it. She didn't mind. TV dinners were a treat because Grandma Welker never had them in the house; Grandma had thought they were totally worthless and tasteless.

Maybe some of them were, but the Mexican ones were delicious. This one had had a cheese enchilada and refried beans and Spanish rice and a tamale. The tamale was the best, but it was very small; Katie had eaten it in three bites. She wondered if they made dinners that had more tamales.

It was warm, but Katie didn't feel like swimming any more even if there was someone in the pool. She could see, through the sliding glass doors that looked out onto the deck, that there were people down there. Mr. P. and Miss K. were stretched out in the lounge chairs, and Mr. C. was there on the edge of the pool again.

They all wore bathing suits, but they weren't swimming. They were talking, and Katie felt a prickle of apprehension. Were they talking about her?

She suddenly decided to see if she could find out. Monica was silent in her darkened bedroom. Nathan hadn't showed up, for the first evening since Katie had come to live with her mother. She wondered if Monica's headache was because she'd had a quarrel with Nathan, but she didn't want to ask.

She couldn't go down the stairs from the deck without being seen, but she could take the inner stairs and then go out through a door that the manager used, at one corner of the pool area. The people who lived on the ground floor used that door, too. It came out a short distance behind where the two men and Miss K. were sitting.

It was also shielded from them by another one of those bonsai trees; this one was a little bigger than the ones nearer the pool. Katie thought if she opened the door very quietly and moved slowly in her bare feet, she could crouch behind the tree and hear what the three were saying.

And just as she'd suspected, they were talking about *her*.

She could see them through the prickly little tree, bits and pieces of them. Mr. Cooper was facing almost toward her, but he was looking at Miss K. Miss K., in an electric blue bikini, was worth looking at.

She poked at her red-gold curls and said, "I think you're both crazy. She's just a normal little girl."

"Then how come," Mr. P. said, leaning forward, "she made that rock jump out and whack me on the ankle? You saw the rock!"

"I didn't see it leap out and hit you," Miss K. said. "I only saw it there after you'd hurt your ankle."

Mr. P. struck the arm of the lounge chair with his fist. "I tell you, that kid is dangerous! She can make things happen; I *know* she can!"

"Well, I don't believe that," Miss K. said. "But even if she *could,* you brought it on yourself. You were nasty to her."

"Nasty! Because I was annoyed when she ran into me and spilled my insurance applications all down the stairs, and then walked on them? Do you know how long it took to fix them up so they were fit to take to the office? And I had to go back to some of my clients and have them sign new copies. Listen, obviously Mr. Cooper realizes there is something mighty peculiar about that kid, or he wouldn't be asking about her!"

Katie was getting a cramp in her back from hunching down to keep out of sight, but she didn't dare move.

Miss K. turned her head so that Katie could see her profile. "Well, why are you asking questions about her, Mr. Cooper? She hasn't done anything to you, has she?"

"Not a thing," Adam Cooper said.

"Well, she hasn't to *me*, either, and Mrs. Michaelmas thinks she's cute, too, so why are we wasting time talking about all this silliness? I'm going to swim."

For a moment, after Miss K. got up from the lounge chair, neither of the men said anything. They were too busy looking at Miss K. to notice that Katie crept back inside through the service door.

She wasn't imagining things. Mr. C. really was investigating her in some way, and for some particular purpose.

It wasn't until the next time Katie eavesdropped that she learned what Mr. C. was after, and then she found that it was even more frightening than she had supposed.

Katie returned to the apartment to find that Monica had emerged from her bedroom and was sitting at the kitchen table, looking wan and pale and sipping iced tea.

She looked up and tried to smile. "Hi. Want to join me in a cold drink?"

Katie shook her head. "Do you feel better?"

"A little," Monica said. "You didn't take any phone calls while I was asleep, did you?"

"No. Did you think Nathan would call?"

Monica grimaced. "I guess I hoped he might. On the other hand, *he* was the one who started the quarrel, and I'm not sure I even want him to call. I never realized how jealous he was, how unreasonable. If I can't even talk to a neighbor when he's right there, why I'd be foolish to get any more deeply involved with him. I had one marriage that didn't work out; I don't want another one."

"Are you going to marry Nathan?" Katie asked carefully.

"No." Monica drank deeply of the iced tea and sighed. "No, I am not going to marry Nathan, although I was considering it. I'm beginning to see that Nathan and I are not suited to each other at all. Sometimes I wonder if I'm suited to anyone, but it's so lonely, being all by yourself."

Katie knew all about that. She was relieved to hear that Nathan wasn't going to become a member of the family, and she wondered how long it would take for the tobacco smell to wear off the living room furniture.

"Do you like Mr. Cooper?" she asked.

"Oh, I suppose he's a nice man. I really haven't seen enough of him to know, for sure," Monica said. "Don't get any ideas about matchmaking, Katie. I'll find someone again, one of these days."

"Do you ever hear from Daddy?"

"From Joe? No, I haven't seen or heard from him in a long time. Katie, you don't dream about us getting back together, do you? Because it won't happen, honey. I know it would be lovely for you, if we were all a family again. But when a marriage is over, it's over. We couldn't hold it together for your sake before, even though we both knew you needed a family, because it was bad for us. Do you understand that?"

"I guess so," Katie said. But she didn't really understand. While she supposed she'd known, in the back of her mind, that her parents would never be married to each other again, she knew she'd sort of hoped that it *might* happen. It was just one of those dreams kids have, like being able to fly. You think it would be fun, but you don't really believe in it.

Monica didn't look as if she felt much like talking, and Katie didn't, either. Or, rather, Katie *did* feel like talking, only there was no one she could talk to. Other people, she thought, had mothers they could talk to about their intimate problems. But she was too afraid of what Monica's face would look like if she suddenly learned that Adam Cooper was asking so many questions about her, and why. If Monica was afraid of a baby that didn't cry, and then uncomfortable because that child taught herself to read at the age of three, how would she feel to know that her daughter was able to communicate with cats, make small objects move through the air without touching them, and create winds all by herself, violent winds that could slam a door hard enough to make a man's nose bleed when it struck him?

No, talking to Monica was out of the question. Katie left her sitting there sipping her tea, looking rather sad and lost. Much the way Katie felt. She went to her room to read, but fell asleep puzzling over her problem.

Her anxiety was still with her the next morning, and after puzzling a long time she decided that there was one person she could talk to: Mrs. M. She would at least be honest. Katie let herself out into the corridor, but she didn't knock on Mrs. M.'s door.

The reason for that was that the door stood ajar, and she could see that there was no one inside the apartment except Lobo, who was polishing off something in his cat dish. He lifted his head and stared at her, his great yellow eyes unblinking.

"Hi, Lobo. Where's Mrs. M.?"

She didn't really expect an answer, but it was there, hanging in her mind almost as if the cat had spoken. Mrs. M. had gone downstairs to mail a letter.

Oh. That explained why she'd left the door open; she expected to be right back and didn't want to bother with a key.

"Are you all well now?" Katie asked politely.

Lobo switched his tail, as if to convey the information that sick cats didn't eat. He licked at his dish.

Katie turned away, heading for the stairs. She *had* to talk to somebody. She was on the landing, halfway down to the ground floor foyer, when she heard their voices. Mrs. M. and Mr. C.

"Look," Mrs. M. said crossly, "who are you, anyway? What do you have against that little girl?"

"I don't have anything against her, I only want some information, and I think you can give it to me, Mrs. Michaelmas. Katie has confided in you."

"She trusts me. That's because I don't go blabbing everything I know," Mrs. M. said, her voice heavy with meaning.

Mr. C. didn't back off, however. He wasn't discouraged. Either he was thick-skinned, which Katie didn't think he was, or it was important to him to get answers; otherwise, he wouldn't have kept pushing when Mrs. M. had made it clear she thought he was too nosey.

Katie tiptoed down another step so that she could look over the railing and see them, or at least the tops of their heads. Mrs. M.'s white hair looked as if someone had stirred it up with an eggbeater, wisps going in all directions.

Mr. C. ran a hand through his thick sandy thatch and spoke with a quiet firmness. "Mrs. Michaelmas, I'm afraid Katie's in trouble. You can help her, by helping me."

"In trouble?" Mrs. M.'s voice sharpened, and Katie felt her own stomach bunch up into an uncomfortable knot. "What are you talking about? What kind of trouble?"

"Has she talked to you about her grandmother?"

"I know she lived with her grandmother for a few years, that's all."

"Did she say anything to you about how her grandmother died?"

Katie's fingers curled on the stair railing, and although it was still warm, she felt a chill. What did he mean?

"The people who live across the road from her grandmother's place think Katie is responsible for a lot of bad things that have happened on their farm. Young pigs born dead, fruit falling off the trees before it's ripe, Mr. Armbruster breaking his arm when the ladder slipped out from under him."

Mrs. M. made a rude noise. "Pish! How silly can you get? Katie's a sweet child; she wouldn't harm anyone!"

"Well, that's what you think. Some of her grandmother's neighbors think otherwise. And they say that Mrs. Welker was afraid of her granddaughter because of things that Katie knew how to do. Things most kids never even thought of doing, and things other people, even adults, can't do. You wouldn't believe the stories I heard in that little town about Katie's peculiar activities."

"No, I wouldn't," Mrs. M. said stoutly. If Katie hadn't been so perturbed by what Mr. C. was saying, she'd have spared a moment to bless Mrs. M.

"Well, some people in Delaney think Katie's a sort of witch. If she'd been around a few hundred years ago, they'd probably have burned her at the stake or drowned her on a dunking stool. And it isn't just the people where she used to live, Mrs. Michaelmas. Surely you're aware that some odd things have happened right here, in this building, since Katie moved in."

Katie scarcely listened while he listed the events surrounding Mr. Pollard. Her fright had grown until it was making her shake. She'd read in school about the old days when witches were burned or tied to a stool that was used to hold them under water in an attempt to make them confess that they were witches. If a person didn't drown, Mrs. Anderson had explained, that proved to the villagers that that person was a witch, because how else could she have lived after being dunked and held under? And, of course, if the "witch" drowned, proving that she had not had supernatural powers after all, why, that was too bad. They'd simply made a mistake.

They didn't still do things like that to people they thought were witches. But what *might* they do, if they were afraid of her? Afraid of what she could do?

Up to now, her powers to create winds and move things about had been part nuisance and part entertainment. Now, Katie saw quite clearly that they could also be incredibly dangerous. And unfortunately, the powers were so small, so weak, that they didn't give her any protection against those who might want to harm her because she was different.

Mr. Armbruster, she thought furiously. She'd had nothing to do with his pigs and had only made fruit drop a few days sooner than it would have fallen, anyway. She certainly hadn't made his ladder fall over so that he broke his arm. She could see that she ought not to have had anything to do with him at all; it had been a serious mistake to entertain herself by stirring up winds around him that blew the leaves off the trees so that they drifted onto the lawn he'd just raked, and by rolling apples under his feet so that he'd skidded on them.

Mr. and Mrs. Armbruster had been in church the times the papers had slithered around, too, and everybody had started sneezing. Mrs. Armbruster had sneezed so hard that the flowers on her hat went askew, and her face had been red before she stopped. Katie had never especially liked them because they were always cross and short-tempered and had forbidden her ever to pick any more of the blackberries along their fences. That was quite unreasonable, in Katie's opinion, because the bushes were on the *outside* of the fences along the road, and mostly Mrs. Armbruster didn't even pick them all for her own use.

They had never been able to understand where the berries went after Katie learned that she could sit on the far side of the road and pluck them through the air, one by one, sailing them directly into her opened mouth.

That had been mildly entertaining until the time when she had almost sucked in a bee by mistake, thinking it was a berry. She'd realized her error just in time, and luckily the bewildered bee had chosen to return to its honey-filled blossom rather than teach her a lesson with its sting.

And now those horrid Armbrusters were saying something bad about her. Katie sank onto the stairs and pressed her face against the stair railing. Mrs. M. knew a lot of things about her, and if Mrs. M. wasn't a real friend, she could certainly fill Mr. C.'s ears with what he wanted to hear.

Mrs. M. was standing now with her hands on her wide hips, scrunching up the most wildly flowered muumuu Katie had yet seen, glaring at Mr. C.

"Look, I've got better things to do than listen to what some idiot farmer thinks about a perfectly nice little girl. I don't know what you think you're up to, moving in here and pretending to make friends with her, but don't expect any help from me in causing trouble for her."

"I'm not trying to cause any trouble, Mrs. Michaelmas. I'm trying to straighten out the trouble that's already there. I can see I'm going to have to show you this."

Katie heard Mrs. M.'s indrawn breath and pressed

harder against the bars in an effort to see what it was Mr. C. was showing her. It was small, because he held it in his hand; he must have taken it from his pocket.

Mrs. M. reacted like a balloon with a slow leak. She seemed to shrink in size, as the air and the antagonism seeped out of her.

Katie could see the woman's face, and it look frightened now, rather than angry. When she spoke, Mrs. M.'s voice was unsteady. "What do you want of me?"

"I want to know what that child can do. Make things move, make winds blow, that kind of thing."

Katie held her breath. Beside her, Lobo appeared on silent cat feet, his amber eyes gleaming. When he leaned against her, Katie put a hand on his soft fur simply from habit—she'd always liked cats, even before she found out they could talk to her—but her attention was still on the scene below her.

"What do you want with a little girl who isn't even ten years old yet?" Mrs. M. asked. "She isn't much more than a baby."

"Some people think she's a very dangerous baby," Mr. C. said in a quiet voice that just barely carried to the listener on the stairs. "Her old neighbors think the police should investigate how her grandma came to fall down those cellar steps and die in the fall. Surely you can see why it's important to learn the truth?"

Katie was unaware of drawing the big cat into her arms, unaware of the solid furry weight of him.

They thought she'd killed her grandma? Was that what they thought? How could anyone believe such a terrible thing?

Katie felt as if she were suffocating.

"You must be crazy, or those neighbors are," Mrs. M.

116

said, but she sounded as weak as Katie felt.

"Now you see why I have to know about Katie," Mr. C. said. "Let's go upstairs, Mrs. Michaelmas, where we can talk in private."

Upstairs. Katie heard that word and rose silently to her feet and fled, carrying Lobo with her.

II

SHE DIDN'T realize, until she'd locked the apartment door behind her, that she had Mrs. M.'s cat.

He was warm and comforting against her chest, but there was no real comfort in him. Lobo couldn't help her.

It wouldn't do any good to be locked inside the apartment, either. The manager had a key, and they could come after her. Besides Monica would let them in when she came home, if the manager didn't.

What was she going to do?

Would Mrs. M. tell him how she could manipulate objects without touching them? Mr. P. would, of course. He'd already talked about the wind slamming the door into his face, and his briefcase coming open, and the rock that hit his foot; and of course Mr. C. had come on the scene when Mr. P.'s money was blowing around when there was no wind anywhere else.

Would they arrest her? They didn't burn witches at the stake any more, or use that dreadful dunking stool, but they locked up people if they thought they'd killed someone.

Could they seriously believe she'd done something like that to her grandma? Would they take her to trial, to prove it one way or the other?

How could they prove anything? They might prove that she had played silly tricks, the ones in church and the ones on the neighbors, but she couldn't prove she'd had nothing to do with Grandma Welker falling down the stairs.

She supposed the Armbrusters had told Mr. C. about the incident shortly before the accident happened. They'd all been there, in Grandma's back yard, and they knew Grandma Welker was angry because Katie hadn't done her chores while her grandma was in town, the way she'd been instructed to do. When the Armbrusters brought her home and Grandma found the kitchen still a mess, Grandma Welker had spoken quite crossly.

Katie had not intended to disobey. She'd simply been absorbed in a fascinating book called *Jack-in-the-Box Planet*, about a boy named Willie who had a robot who was supposed to be his servant but who had actually become his jailer. And as often happened when Katie became immersed in a book, she forgot about everything else.

So she had been sitting on the porch swing, eating from a bowl of cherries and making a little pile of pits beside her on the floor, when Grandma's cross voice brought her back to reality.

"I've told you and told you," Grandma said through tight lips, "not to make a mess with pits on the porch."

Still only halfway out of the world of Willie and his

119

Major-Domo, Katie had acted without thinking. She slid the pits off the edge of the porch and tumbled them through the grass.

The Armbrusters, behind her, didn't see that, but Katie's grandma did. She didn't mention the cherry pits, however, but asked about the dishes. Had Katie cleaned up the kitchen and washed and dried the dishes?

Katie swallowed. "I forgot them. But I'll do them right now."

She almost ran into the house, taking the precious book with her; she still had a few pages to read, and she wanted to know as quickly as possible how it came out, but she knew she had to do it when her grandma wasn't watching. Grandma didn't value books all that much; she'd even burned one, once, when she'd caught Katie reading it after she was supposed to have been asleep. Katie had had difficulty in forgiving her for that. She'd had to fish the remains out of the fireplace late that night and carefully lay out the brown pages with the charred edges to find out how it ended.

Grandma Welker's voice had floated after her. "I don't know what I'm going to do with that child. The next time Monica comes, or Joe calls, I'm going to have to tell them I'm getting too old to cope with a child like Katie."

She hadn't listened to the rest of it. The Armbrusters and her grandma had stood there talking, however, for at least ten minutes before Grandma Welker came inside, and she still looked upset and angry.

And, half an hour later, she'd cried out and pitched down those steep cellar steps and hit her head on something.

Katie had been very frightened. She'd gone to the

telephone and called for help. The ambulance, first, because obviously her grandma was seriously hurt. And then she'd called Mr. Tanner, and when he came a few minutes later (he only lived a short distance down the road, so he got there before the ambulance did), he told her, very gently, that her grandma was dead. He had taken her home with him, and he'd called Monica, and taken care of the things that had to be done. He'd even remembered to take along Dusty, and had promised to give the old dog a home for as long as he lived, there on the Tanner's little farm.

And now, Katie thought, looking around the apartment where she had lived for such a short time, now the police were after her because they thought she'd pushed her grandma down those stairs. Mr. C. must be a policeman, mustn't he? Why else would his identification have scared Mrs. M. into cooperating with him? The Armbrusters must have said something to the police, those wicked, wicked Armbrusters, who had no reason to think anything of the sort.

You're hurting me.

The words came to her mind as if they'd been spoken, though of course Lobo hadn't said a word. He hadn't even meowed.

"I'm sorry." Katie relaxed her hold, still cradling him against her. She had never cried, and she didn't cry now; the tears were there in her voice, however. "Lobo, what am I going to do? I couldn't bear it if they locked me up."

Would Monica stop them, or try to stop them, from putting her in jail? Or would Monica think that was where she belonged?

"She might. She thinks I'm peculiar, too; and if she

gets the idea I had anything to do with Grandma falling down the stairs . . . if only I had someone to talk to, someone like my father. I don't think *he'd* let them lock me up, but I don't know where he is . . ."

Katie sank onto the nearest chair, stroking Lobo's head and back, trying to think. She had no one to turn to, no one to help her.

Unless . . .

What about those other children? The ones who might be like her? Would they be able to help? Would they understand?

They seemed her only hope.

She had no way of knowing, of course, whether just because those other kids had been born the same month as she had, they would be like her. Or that they would help her. Yet she did know that Kerri Lamont was different, too; surely Kerri would understand what was happening to Katie. Kerri might not be able to do anything about it, but Katie didn't know what else to do. Finding the other children seemed the only possible action she could take.

She must have been squeezing him too hard again; Lobo suddenly pushed against her and leaped down, and she opened the door for him into the corridor. She didn't see either Mrs. M. or Mr. C. when Lobo slipped silently through the crack. He scratched at the opposite door, meowing loudly, and Katie closed her own door before anyone could see her.

Did she dare to stay here in the apartment? Was it safe, now that Mr. C. had openly revealed himself as a police officer investigating her grandmother's death? He wasn't ready to arrest her yet, at least she didn't think he was, but how could she be sure of anything?

Probably he wouldn't take her away before her mother came home, unless he became convinced that she was really dangerous. Then he might. What had Mrs. M. told him? If she admitted the things she knew Katie could do, would that evidence count against her even though it was all perfectly harmless? And if they brought her to trial, how could she possibly prove she hadn't done a particular thing? There had been nobody in the house except herself and Grandma Welker, and old Dusty. Maybe Dusty had seen Grandma fall, although mostly what he did these days was sleep, the way old dogs did, so it was hard to tell about that. Certainly Dusty couldn't help her. Nobody could help her, except maybe those other kids.

She had to find them.

Katie spoke slowly, aloud to herself. "I think I'll go try to find that Dale Casey. I have his address. And then maybe when I come home, Mrs. M. will tell me if it's safe to stay here in the apartment."

It wasn't much of a plan, but it was the best she could think of at the moment.

She was still worried and frightened, but now that she had a plan, she didn't feel quite so desperate. She got the slip of paper with the names and addresses on it and put it in the pocket of her blue shorts, along with the contents of her bank, which came to six dollars and fourteen cents. Then she thought she ought to fortify herself against what might be a long spell with nothing to eat.

She cut herself opening a can of tuna fish and wrapped a piece of tissue around her finger until it stopped bleeding. Even so, it wasn't easy to make sandwiches without bleeding on them. She ate one and wrapped the other one to carry with her. While hunting for something else that would be easy to carry, she found a Hershey bar and put that into the Baggie with the second sandwich.

The cut was still bleeding and she decided the tissue wasn't helping much. Maybe if she put a Band-Aid on it, tightly so that it held the edges of the cut together, the bleeding would stop.

Katie wondered if she ought to leave a note for Monica, in case she didn't come home before her mother did, and decided against it. What could she say that wouldn't incriminate her, if Mr. C. saw it?

If she was lucky, she'd find a way to come home safely, and Monica would never know she'd been away. If she was unlucky, well, a note might just lead the police to her sooner, because if she mentioned any names, Monica might well tell them where those kids lived, and they'd look there.

She decided, in the interest of saving time, to take the city bus to Dale Casey's house. It only cost thirty cents and would save her a long walk.

She hadn't ridden on a bus very often before, and she felt strange climbing aboard and dropping her coins into the little box beside the driver. He didn't pay any attention to her, though, not even to notice that her eyes were silver-colored.

Katie sat next to a window, watching the other passengers and the scenery. The bus went through a business section, and a lot of people got on and off. Most of them were women with shopping bags, and a few were old men. None of them paid any attention to Katie, except a boy about her own age who sat across the aisle and tried to hit the back of the bus driver's neck with spitballs. He wasn't very good at it, but Katie thought it would be best if there was no commotion while she was aboard; in case Mr. C. ever asked any questions of the bus driver, she saw to it that the spitballs, made from old gum wrappers, went everywhere except where the boy was trying to put them. One accidentally landed in the hair of a lady with a bulging shopping bag, and Katie hastily made it slide off the blue-rinsed curls into the bag with a naked chicken and a package of spaghetti sticking out of it.

The boy glanced at her suspiciously, although he couldn't possibly know she had anything to do with his failures, could he? Katie stared back, her face carefully blank, and reached up with a finger to push her glasses back up onto her nose. She was proud of herself, that she'd remembered to do it with her finger.

She was glad when the boy got off the bus. He was the only one who'd even so much as looked at her.

She got off at the corner where Mrs. M. had told her to leave the bus. It was on the edge of a nice residential area, with shading trees and flowers and well-kept yards.

There were also dogs.

When an ugly little cur came dashing out at her, yapping furiously, from the porch of a big, comfortable-looking house, Katie decided it was time to find out for certain if she could communicate with dogs as well as cats.

"Go back on the porch at once," Katie told him, "or I'll bring the dog catcher to pick you up and put you in the pound."

The dog, which had a long tail and floppy ears and short hair between the two ends of himself, shuddered to an abrupt halt.

"Have you ever been in a pound?" Katie demanded.

"Do you know what it's like?"

The animal's expression was so funny she might have laughed if she hadn't been so perturbed about her own situation. No doubt he was trained as a watch dog, and he thought he was doing his duty.

"Well, at least wait until someone steps on your property. Don't bark at people on the sidewalk," Katie told him, and walked on leaving the dog looking after her in a bewildered way.

It was a warm day, and she was afraid the Hershey bar would melt, so she took it out and ate it. She was licking the chocolate from her fingers when she found the address she'd written down, the place where Dale Casey lived.

It was a nice big house with a large lawn. Katie hesitated, then gathered her courage and walked up to the front door and rang the bell.

When the chimes ended, the door opened, and there he was.

She knew him at once, because his eyes looked just like hers.

Dale Casey, like Katie, wore glasses. And behind the lenses were eyes a mirror-image of her own. Silver eyes.

Behind him, from the interior of the house, a woman's voice demanded, "Who is it, Dale? Don't go anywhere; you know Daddy will be home any minute, and he wants you to be ready to go to Grandma's for dinner."

For a moment the boy's gaze locked with Katie's in wordless recognition. Then he turned his head and spoke over his shoulder. "It's OK, Mom, I'm going to be right in the front yard."

He lowered his voice to an urgent whisper. "I can't talk to you now; we're leaving for my grandma's birthday party. It's going to last practically all weekend, but I'll be home Sunday night. Can you come back Sunday night?"

Sunday night loomed light-years away. Katie moistened her lips, not sure what she intended to say. She was torn between disappointment and triumph; she had found him, one of those September children, but already he was slipping away from her, for at least a few more days. She wouldn't have minded so much except that she really needed help at once.

"I tried to call you a couple of times," Dale Casey said. He was a serious-looking boy with fair hair and a smattering of freckles, as if he'd walked beneath a ladder when someone was applying tan paint and it had sprinkled on him. "Only it's impossible to have a private telephone conversation in this house. They always want to know who you're talking to, or what you're saying, or want you to get off the line because they're waiting for an important call. How did you know about me? Can you read minds?"

Katie blinked, startled. "Maybe cats, a little. Can you read people's?"

"Sometimes. Some of them." She saw her own excitement rising in the boy's face. "Are there more of us? Or only us two?"

"I don't know. I think maybe there are two more. A girl named Kerri Lamont and a boy named Eric Van-Allsburg. I haven't found them yet—at least, Kerri lives in Millersburg, but I haven't met her. And Eric's mother has remarried and I don't know her new name."

"Can you—" Dale began, and then the door behind him, which he had pulled almost shut, was suddenly jerked open and a woman stood there. She was pretty, and dressed to go out; she started to speak to her son and then stopped.

Katie felt her stomach muscles tightening when Mrs. Casey looked into her face. No, into her eyes.

She had been smiling, pleasant, and now she was not smiling at all. She looked alarmed, maybe even frightened. "Who's your friend, Dale?"

"Uh, Katie, uh . . ."

"Katie Welker," Katie said, taking an instinctive step backward.

"I don't remember you ever mentioning a Katie Welker before—oh! Is this the little girl who called you on the phone the other day?"

There was disapproval in Mrs. Casey's tone, and Katie wasn't sure whether it was because she'd called Dale or because of the way she looked. Silver eyes.

"Where do you come from?" Mrs. Casey asked; and when Katie went to retreat one more step, the woman put out a hand on her shoulder. Not roughly, but firmly, so that Katie felt trapped like a wild animal, and her heart was beating as if she were indeed caught in a trap. "Welker? Monica Welker's child?"

The fingers on her shoulder tightened, and Katie panicked. She pulled loose from Mrs. Casey and ran, nearly colliding with the man getting out of a car at the curb.

"Stop her! Al, stop that child!"

The voice behind her, the startled grunt as Mr. Casey swung around, served to make Katie feel as if she were a thief, running from the scene of her crime.

"Look at her eyes!" Mrs. Casey cried, and again Katie felt a hand descend on her shoulder.

"Here, what's going on?" Mr. Casey asked.

But before he could get a firm grip, Katie twisted and

ran, ran as fast as she'd ever run in her life.

If he had chased her, of course, he probably would have caught up with her. He didn't, though; and after Katie had cut through a yard where an old woman was watering her flowers and had plunged through a hole in a hedge leading onto a side street, she was able to slow her pace.

She was breathing rapidly and painfully. There was an oozing scratch on her bare arm where the hedge had torn her skin, and she had to stop for a moment, both to get her breath and figure out where she was. Which way did she go to return to the bus line?

People were coming home from work. It must be later than she'd thought. A man with a dinner pail parked his car, looked at her with mild curiosity, and went on up the walk into a house.

Katie's breathing slowed, and she walked toward what she thought was the right street to catch the bus. She had made a mistake, however, and had to turn around and walk back the other way, before she, at last, saw the Bus Stop sign.

It wasn't the place where she'd gotten off, and there was no bus in sight. Katie glanced around to make sure that no one was following her and saw that she was on the edge of a small park. There were plenty of people around, but no one was paying any attention to her.

She saw a fountain in the park, at the point where two paths crossed, so she walked over to it and sat on the cement edge of the pool around it. The water made a pleasant tinkling sound. She dipped a hand into the pool and wondered if anyone would think it odd if she splashed some of it over her face to cool herself.

An old man was feeding pigeons, who flocked around

him as he sat on a green bench. And beyond him, some boys were playing. Katie sat resting, wondering what Dale Casey's parents had meant to do to her. *Look at her eyes*, Mrs. Casey had said. Nobody could lock you up because of the color of your eyes, could they? Would they try to find her, though? Or would they just forget about her?

Katie rinsed the blood off her arm where she'd scratched it, biting her lip at the way the water made it sting. If only she knew how Monica would react if someone came after her, either the Caseys or the police. Would Monica protect her, or would she be glad to be rid of her? It was dreadful, not knowing.

"Hey! Give it back! It belongs to us!"

The shout brought Katie around to look at two boys who were throwing a Frisbee back and forth, and she was reminded of the time Jack Salforth and Donnie Edwards had teased her by tossing one of her shoes from one to the other over her head. They were new shoes, and she had known her grandma would be furious if one of them was lost. Katie had at last given up on the boys tiring of their teasing and when the school bus came, she'd resorted to redirecting the shoe, sailing it in through a bus window beside a girl who'd handed it back to her as she got on. The boys had been stunned, since neither of them had intended to throw it through the bus window, and they hadn't tried to take it away from her again.

So now she knew how the small boys felt as their Frisbee sailed out of their reach. She watched for a minute, and had just about decided to make the Frisbee sail away from the older boys and into the pool beside her, where the little boys could retrieve it, when something happened to the big plastic disk.

The taller of the two tormentors hurled it, laughing, but instead of passing over the heads of its owners to the other tall boy, the Frisbee dipped and swirled and returned, like a boomerang, to smack the thrower in the mouth.

The boy let out a startled yelp and clapped his hand to his teeth, then stared in amazement at the blood on his fingers. And then the Frisbee, seemingly with a mind of its own, swooped toward the second tormentor and clipped him sharply on the ear. It seemed to Katie that it would have hit *him* in the face, as well, if he hadn't dodged at the crucial moment.

This boy, too, cried out in pain and rubbed at his injured ear. Then the Frisbee dropped onto the grass in front of the boy who owned it.

"Come on, let's go play somewhere else," he said, and he and his friend moved quickly away from the two bullies.

The two tall boys stood in bewilderment, wondering what had happened to them. But Katie had already forgotten them. She was looking around to see who was there, who might, like herself, have decided to help the Frisbee in its flight pattern.

Only two people were paying any attention to the boys. One was the old man feeding the pigeons, who had momentarily forgotten the birds. The other was a boy walking a dog on a leash.

It was at the boy that Katie stared. Her breath caught in her throat. For although he was tall, he *might* be no more than ten years old. He was dark-haired, and he wore horn-rimmed glasses much like Katie's; he was too far away for her to be sure of the color of his eyes, but the growing excitement within her made her almost convinced that they were silver like her own.

The dog was an Airedale, a great shaggy, friendly-looking animal, who tugged at the leash. Now he lunged forward, and the boy allowed himself to be dragged along the path.

At that very moment, Katie heard the bus coming. She stood up, looking first toward the bus, and then toward the boy and the Airedale moving rapidly away from her. Which was more important, to know for sure about the boy, or to catch the bus?

It wasn't a difficult decision to make. Katie took several steps after the boy and cried out. "Wait! Please, wait!"

The boy turned to glance over his shoulder, obviously startled, and then broke into a run. Away from her, not toward her. With the Airedale getting into the spirit of it, the two of them fairly flew away and disappeared behind some low shrubs. By the time Katie reached the curb and looked around the corner, the boy and the dog had vanished.

She was breathing quickly, the disappointment sharp in her chest, an actual pain. He had to have done it, the business with the Frisbee, didn't he? Someone had, and he was the right age, and the only one nearby.

He was gone now, though. Katie turned back toward the bus, which had stopped for the old man who'd been feeding the pigeons. She climbed aboard after him, dropping her coins into the box and sinking into a seat halfway back in the bus. If only she'd caught up with him! Was he one of them, the September children? One like herself and Dale Casey? She had no doubts at all that Dale was as different from normal kids as she was. Only she didn't quite see how to make contact with him without his parents knowing it; and after the way they'd reacted to her today, she was afraid of them.

And this other boy, could he possibly be Eric Van-Allsburg? She wondered if he came often to the park, if she'd see him again if she returned. Even if he wasn't one of the kids on her list, Katie decided he had to be the one who'd made that Frisbee move the way it did. *She* hadn't done it, although she'd intended to do *something*. And the boy with the big dog was the only one, except Katie and the man with the pigeons, who'd been paying any attention.

She looked across the aisle at that old man now and saw that he was tired and shabby-looking. He met her gaze, and his eyes were blue. He smiled a little, and Katie tried to smile back.

No, *he* wasn't responsible for giving the Frisbee a life of its own. It was the other one. Eric. Maybe he was Eric. She'd have to go back to the park, in case he walked his dog there again. She'd have to find out for sure. If Mr. C. and the Caseys didn't do something to stop her.

Katie's seat mate was a fat lady whose shopping bag, with queen-size pantyhose and a package of hamburger showing at the top of it, took up almost all the leg room. The lady didn't offer to move it, and Katie didn't ask her to. She simply sat, taking up as little space as she could and listening to the two women ahead of her talk about how their feet hurt and how warm it was.

Katie didn't know whether she ought to go home or not. She wasn't even sure she'd recognize the right corner, so she decided to ride on past and get off at the following corner. That way she could sneak around through the back alley and sort of reconnoiter, in case Mr. C. had laid a trap for her.

She came around the side of the building and saw that Miss K.'s blue Pinto was in the parking lot. Did that mean it was late enough for Monica to be home, wondering what had happened to her?

Katie wished she could talk to Mrs. M. before she went upstairs. She was very hungry; she hadn't even gotten to eat the second sandwich she'd carried with her. It had been lost during her dash away from the Casey house.

There was a lot of shrubbery along the side of the building, which provided some cover as Katie worked her way toward the parking lot. Mr. C.'s car was there, too, though he himself was not in sight.

There was a familiar figure nearby, however. Just as she reached the front corner of the building, partially screened by some very prickly evergreen shrubs, Mr. P. came out of the front door. Miss K. was right behind him, but Katie didn't get the idea they were together. Miss K. had on a lovely pale blue summer dress and a jangly bracelet; she looked as if she were going to a party. Mr. P. was wearing slacks and tennis shoes and a T-shirt.

"Yes," Miss K. said clearly, "I got my paper, all right. The boy left it in front of my door, the same as always."

"Well, he didn't leave mine. I wondered if he dropped it out here somewhere. Either that or someone swiped it." Mr. P. stood on the front walk looking around, and Katie held very still behind the bushes.

"Isn't that him coming now? Yes, it is. Maybe he ran out of papers or something and had to go home for more.

Well, I have to run. Bye-bye," Miss K. said, and crossed the paving toward her car.

Sure enough, when Katie shifted position slightly she could see Jackson Jones. He parked his bike and called out, "Hi, Mr. Pollard! Could I collect for the paper?"

Mr. P. stared at him. "You just collected! What are you talking about? How many times a week do you have to get paid?"

"Just once, if you'd pay me the first time I come. That was for last week's paper that you paid me, Mr. Pollard. Now you owe me for this week's."

Mr. P. scowled. "That can't be right! I'm sure I paid you for this week."

Jackson Jones held his ground. "No, sir. If you'll check your receipt, you'll see that it has the dates right on it."

"I didn't even get a paper tonight. Do I have to pay for papers you don't deliver?"

"No, sir. I was short one paper tonight, and I knew I had to come back later to collect, anyway, so I brought the paper with me." Jackson Jones handed it over, and Mr. P. didn't look any happier to have it. "Could you pay me now for this week, sir?"

Katie could see that he wasn't going to do it. Forgetting her own situation for a moment, she began to work at Mr. P.'s wallet, but he put a hand over his back pocket and she couldn't get the wallet out. She changed tactics then, and concentrated on the newspaper held loosely under his arm. He wasn't anticipating that, and Katie flipped the paper away from him and out onto the lawn, where the sprinkler was running.

Mr. P. swore, dashed for the already soggy paper, and grabbed too late at his back pocket. The wallet, once it had fallen onto the sidewalk, was easy enough to open.

When a single bill had slithered out and Jackson Jones had placed his foot on it, Katie simply watched and waited.

Mr. P. had turned an unbecoming pink, even on his bald spot. He shook water off the newspaper, swore again, and resigned himself to waiting for Jackson Jones to write out a receipt and make change for the bill still anchored under his foot.

"How do you do that?" Mr. P. demanded.

"Sir?"

"How the devil do you do it? Make winds that blow my wallet open, make the paper land in the sprinkler."

"Me, sir? I didn't do anything." Jackson Jones sounded as innocent as it was possible to be.

"Is it her, then? That kid with the funny eyes? Is *she* doing it?" He looked wildly around, and for a moment stared right into the shrubbery where Katie stood, so that her heart almost stopped. He didn't see her, though.

"Katie? I haven't seen her around today at all," Jackson Jones said. "Here's your receipt, sir. I'll see you again next Friday."

"I suppose so," Mr. P. said ungraciously. "Well, whatever that Cooper fellow is looking for in the way of evidence, I hope he finds it and locks her up. She's a menace to the whole neighborhood. There's the cops now. I suppose it's too much to hope for that they'll take her away."

Katie crouched lower behind the concealing shrubbery. Sure enough, a police car had drawn up at the curb, and a blue-uniformed officer got out and came up the walk.

"Good evening, sir," the officer said.

"Evening. Who you looking for?" Mr. P. asked eagerly.

The officer checked with his small notebook. "Welker. Apartment 2-A?"

"Right up those stairs and turn right," Mr. P. said. "You coming about that kid?"

"Little girl," the officer confirmed. "Have you seen her, sir?"

"Not lately. And it won't bother me too much if I never see her again." Mr. P. slapped the newspaper once more against his leg and shook his head. "How am I supposed to read a wet paper?"

He turned around and went back inside, and the police officer followed him. Katie felt a tremor run through her legs that was worse even than the hunger pangs in her stomach. Up to now she had had at least a faint hope that she'd misunderstood something, that they weren't going to arrest her. Now there didn't appear to be any doubt at all.

For a moment Jackson Jones stood quite still, looking after the men who had entered the building. Then he glanced around and spoke in a low voice.

"Katie? Are you out there?"

For a moment she didn't answer. Did she dare trust him?

But she had to, didn't she? She didn't know where to go, or what to do; all she was sure of was that she wasn't going to let them take her away to jail if she could help it.

Her voice squeaked a little with nervousness. "I'm over here. In the bushes."

He looked around again, began to whistle off-hand-

137

edly, and took a few steps toward her, not looking directly at her hiding place.

"You in trouble?"

"I think so," Katie said.

"Did Mr. Pollard turn you in for something?"

"I think it was Mr. Cooper."

"Him? I thought he seemed like a nice guy. He paid me ahead of time for the paper. Listen, is it true? Did you do those things, make the door slam in his face and his money blow out of his wallet and all that stuff?"

"I guess so."

"How do you do it?" Jackson Jones asked. He didn't sound as if he didn't believe her, and he didn't sound afraid or hostile, either. "I wouldn't mind a few lessons."

"I don't know how I do it," Katie admitted. "I just think about it, and it happens."

Jackson Jones sighed. "I figured it wasn't something you could teach me. Anyway, thanks. It's the easiest I ever got my money out of Mr. Pollard. What are you going to do?"

"I don't know," Katie said again. "I'd run away and hide, if I knew of any place where they wouldn't find me." She sounded small and forlorn.

"You want some help?"

"Where is there to go?"

"Well." He considered that, kicking at a loose rock near the edge of the walk. "They say the best place to hide something is in with a whole bunch of other things just like it. So, a kid would be the least conspicuous in a bunch of kids, right?"

"Where would I find a bunch of kids? Especially at night?"

"At our house." Someone came out of the door of

The Cedars Apartments, and Jackson Jones pretended he was trying to find something he'd dropped; the man didn't even glance at him. When the stranger was out in the middle of the parking lot, Jackson Jones continued. "My little sister Dorothy is having a slumber party tonight. There'll be so many kids in our house, my mother won't notice another one. I'll lend you my sleeping bag."

Katie began to breathe normally again. "Do you think that would work?"

"Why not? The way our house is, you could probably come even when we weren't having a slumber party and she'd never notice you. Well, she'd know you were there, but she'd just think you were a friend of Dorothy's or Carol's. She never knows half the kids who come to our place."

Katie could see the police car between the branches of her shelter. It gave her cold chills. "How will I get away, though? To get to your house?"

"Go back into the alley," Jackson Jones told her. "Turn left and go until you come out on Sixth Street. I'll meet you there, and we can get to my house through the alley. Nobody'll notice us."

So Katie did as he said, and twenty minutes later she was following Jackson Jones through the back door of a big white frame house that smelled of garlic and tomato sauce. Her stomach contracted painfully. She wondered if she'd dare to ask him for something to eat.

There was no one in the kitchen except a big, fluffy white cat, who lifted his head from a feeding dish.

"That's Homer. He's got a brother around somewhere. Henry," Jackson Jones said. "Come on up the back stairs, and we'll get my sleeping bag for you."

They didn't meet anyone, but somewhere in the distance Katie heard a TV playing, girlish voices giggling, and a male voice shouted, "Whoever took my tennis racket, bring it back!"

The stairs opened onto a second floor landing. From there Katie saw assorted bedrooms and a bathroom with a heap of towels on the floor.

"Wow," Jackson Jones said. "If you want to use the bathroom tonight, maybe you better do it now. It isn't very often empty."

She hadn't wanted to say it, but his suggestion was welcome. Katie used the bathroom while Jackson Jones got the sleeping bag, and then he hesitated. "I better get you some pajamas, too. I think Carol's will fit you. Ma might think it's funny if she sees you in the middle of the night in shorts when everybody else is wearing pajamas."

He went into one of the bedrooms and brought back a pair of summer pajamas with a pink and white bunny print on them. They were pretty childish, but Katie thought they'd probably fit.

Just as they reached the head of the stairs—the front ones, this time—a tall, skinny boy came bounding up two steps at a time. He didn't even look at Katie.

"Jackson Jones, did you snitch my tennis racket?"

"No. Where's the rest of the slumber party? Aren't they going to sleep in Dorothy's room?"

"What, and keep the rest of us awake all night? No, Ma said they had to stay in the basement. Where the heck is my tennis racket?"

"Probably under your bed. If you get a shovel and clean it out, maybe you'll find the racket."

The boy pushed past them and Jackson Jones led the way downstairs. Katie caught a glimpse of Mr. and Mrs.

Jones sitting in the living room, both with their feet up, watching TV. Mrs. Jones turned her head.

"Jackson Jones, I told you I wouldn't keep supper hot past the regular time. You'll have to eat it cold. I'm not going to be still serving and washing up all evening."

"It's OK, Ma. I like cold spaghetti," Jackson Jones assured her. "All the rest of the kids downstairs?"

"Yes, and you tell Dorothy that they can make their final raid on the kitchen at eleven. After that, it's lights out and quiet."

"Sure, Ma." Jackson Jones nudged Katie, who had not been at all sure that Mrs. Jones wouldn't question her presence, and they went on through the house, back to the kitchen, and down the stairs to the basement.

The basement was really pretty nice. A big room that took up one whole end of it had been paneled in knotty pine, and there was a rust-colored carpet on the floor and a color television. What appeared to be about twenty giggling little girls were sprawled in sleeping bags, watching TV and eating. Nobody even looked up when Katie and Jackson Jones came down the stairs.

"Here's a good place," Jackson Jones said, spreading out the sleeping bag in a corner a little bit away from the others. "That's my sister Dorothy over there, the one with her front teeth missing. If she asks who you are, say you're a friend of Carol's. That's Carol over there, changing the channel. If *she* asks you, say you're a friend of Dorothy's. I don't know if you'll get any sleep, but at least you're in off the street. Are you hungry?"

Katie admitted that she was.

"OK. I missed supper, too, having to go back to collect from Mr. Pollard. I'll bring you something. Oh,

141

there's another bathroom over there, where you can put on your pajamas."

Katie stood there for a moment, thinking surely someone would challenge her right to be there. Nobody paid any attention to her, though; they were flipping channels on the TV.

And then, suddenly, and to her horror, Katie saw her own face on the television screen.

12

I T W A S her school picture from last year, the one her grandma had had framed for the top of the piano and had sent copies of to both Monica and her father. Now it stared out from the television screen, a small owllike face with horn-rimmed glasses. Katie wondered if she was going to throw up.

"We interrupt this program for a special bulletin," the voice accompanying the picture said. "Katherine Joyce Welker, age nine, is missing. Anyone seeing this child please call the city police at . . ."

Katie didn't hear the number. She clutched the borrowed pajamas against her chest and fled to the little bathroom beneath the stairs.

What could she do now? All those kids, and probably Mr. and Mrs. Jones upstairs, had seen her picture. The house that had seemed a refuge was now a trap.

She was standing there in the darkened bathroom with the door open when Jackson Jones came back downstairs. He was carrying a tray, and seeing that Katie was not sitting on the sleeping bag, he put down the tray and turned to find her behind him.

"What's the matter?"

Katie beckoned to him with a finger before whispering the awful news. "They just had my picture on TV. They said to call the police if anyone saw me."

Jackson Jones whistled and looked at her with one blue eye and one green one. "Wow." He frowned uneasily. "Maybe you better tell me. What did you do?"

"I didn't do anything. They think I killed my grandma, though. They're going to lock me up if I can't prove I didn't do it."

Jackson Jones whistled again and glanced over his shoulder to make sure none of the little girls in the family room were paying any attention. "I thought you just needed a place to hide for one night. But I guess we'll have to make some long-range plans tomorrow. Let me sleep on it, and I'll see what I can think up."

"You aren't going to turn me in?" Katie asked.

"You didn't do anything, did you? So why should I turn you in? There must be some way to prove you're not a criminal."

"But everybody out there saw my picture!"

"Wearing your glasses? Did the picture show you with glasses?"

"Yes. Just like I look now."

"Take the glasses off, then." He reached out and did it for her. "There. That makes you look different. Was your hair the same, too? Maybe you could braid it or something, to be different. Nobody will recognize you if you do that."

So she tried it. Without her glasses, everything more than a foot away became fuzzy, as if she were peering through thick fog. It made her uneasy, not to be able to see very well, yet it was true she did look very different without the glasses. The braids she made weren't especially neat, but they helped, too.

By the time she'd put on Carol Jones's pajamas and came out of the bathroom, she was still nervous but she hoped that she didn't look enough like the picture on the television so that anyone would recognize her before she could figure out what to do next.

Jackson Jones had brought her a plate with cold spaghetti, molded salad, a buttered roll, and some carrot sticks. Katie ate it sitting cross-legged on the sleeping bag, and when her stomach was full she felt better.

The little girls—there were only fifteen of them, when she took time to count—ran around and went past her, giggling, half a dozen times. No one took any particular notice of her, except that one girl passing around potato chips offered her the bowl. Katie took some and munched thoughtfully. Jackson Jones was right that none of them took her to be the girl who was wanted by the police. So probably it was safe to sleep here. But what was she going to do tomorrow, when all the giggling little girls went home?

During the evening Jackson Jones didn't come back. He was still in the house, though, because twice Katie heard someone calling to him.

"Jackson Jones, shut that door!" and "Jackson Jones, you come out of that bathroom or I'm going to tell Ma!"

Katie wasn't quite so lonesome, knowing he was upstairs somewhere.

Besides watching television and whispering and giggling a lot, the little girls at the slumber party ate. And although Katie's sleeping bag was off in a dimly lighted corner, they brought her food, too. Apparently each of them thought she was part of the group, a guest of the Joneses even if none of them knew her.

They brought her soda pop and Twinkies and popcorn and, about ten o'clock, hot dogs fresh from the kitchen. Junk, her grandma would have called it, but it tasted good to Katie.

On the eleven o'clock news, her picture came on again. Somehow she hadn't expected that, and Katie cringed, curling down inside the bag in case anyone looked at her to compare her with the girl on the screen.

No one was paying any attention, though. Dorothy Jones flicked the switch, and the picture of a fair-haired child with horn-rimmed glasses faded into blackness. "Let's don't watch TV any more," she said. "Let's tell stories. Ghost stories!"

Katie listened to the kids talk, feeling much older than they were, although most of them were no more than a year younger than she was. Ghost stories, told in whispers and dramatic voices, would have been fun, if she hadn't been worrying so much about how she was going to elude the police forever. She'd read a story once about some kids who ran away and lived in a boxcar, all by themselves, but she didn't know where there was a boxcar. Besides, she'd need money to buy food and things, and it was hard for a not-quite-ten-year-old to earn money.

At eleven-thirty, after a particularly loud shriek of pretended fear and then a flurry of laughter, a male voice yelled down the cellar stars. "OK, you kids, knock it off now! The rest of us gotta get some sleep!"

Gradually, the slumber party quieted down, and the kids dozed off. Katie did, too, because it had been a long, difficult day. But she continued to worry, even in her sleep.

She thought sure, in the morning, that someone would ask her who she was, but nobody did. All the girls slept late and woke to dress in summer clothes much like Katie's, so she didn't stand out that way. When they all trooped upstairs for breakfast, she decided to go along. She had intended to save her Twinkie for breakfast, in case she had to run again, but she'd rolled over on it during the night and it was pretty flat. Katie decided to stuff it in her pocket for an emergency, and see if Mrs. Jones would ignore her, too, in all that batch of kids.

She did. She was making pancakes for fifteen—no, sixteen—little girls, and was too busy to look at anyone's face. Katie sat with the others around a big oval table and had sausages and pancakes with blueberry syrup and drank a tall glass of orange juice. She didn't know what to do, though, when after breakfast the girls' mothers began arriving to take them and their sleeping bags home.

She was, of course, the last one left. Jackson Jones hadn't showed up, and Katie felt panic rising again within her. Mrs. Jones smiled at her. "Your mother's not here yet? Would you like to sit on the front porch, in the swing, and wait for her? I think Dorothy and Carol are out there with Jenny Evans; you can wait there, too, if you like."

Katie didn't like, but she didn't know how to refuse without calling further attention to herself. She was greatly relieved when she opened the front screen door to see Jackson Jones coming up the steps with his empty paper bag slung over his shoulder.

"Morning delivery on weekends," he told her, easing

the bag onto the porch. "Did you get some breakfast?"

Katie nodded. She wished she dared to put on her glasses; she had to squint to see without them. Carol and Dorothy and their last guest were out on the sidewalk, playing hopscotch, waiting for the final mother to arrive, so Katie and Jackson Jones could talk without being overheard.

He lowered his voice, anyway. "There's a real ruckus at your place," he said.

Katie's heartbeat began to pick up speed.

"Your mother asked me if I'd seen you. She looked terrible, Katie. She'd been crying. Maybe you ought to let her know you're all right."

Katie's throat felt tight. "If I let her know I'm all right, she'll want me to come home. And then they'll arrest me."

"Mr. Cooper asked me if I'd seen you, too."

"What did you tell him?"

"Said I'd seen you yesterday, and that I didn't remember what time it was. That's the truth. I don't have a watch, and I didn't look at a clock after we got home. And Mrs. Michaelmas asked about you, too."

"I guess she must have told Mr. C. what I could do," Katie said, and then belatedly remembered that Jackson Jones wasn't aware of all those things.

"Boy, I wish *I* could do some magic," Jackson Jones said. "Maybe Mr. Pollard would get so he'd pay the first time and save me all those times going back. What else can you do?"

"Not much," Katie said sadly. "Not enough to get myself out of trouble. In fact, that's what got me into trouble in the first place. I didn't hurt anybody, but I guess it scares people when I move things without touching them, and some of them decided I was dangerous. They think I pushed Grandma Welker down the stairs, but I didn't."

"Anybody'd who'd think a thing like that would have to be pretty stupid," Jackson Jones said. "Could you move that beer can somebody dropped in the street?"

Katie turned and saw the silvery can lying in the gutter. She flipped it along, rolling, until it jumped the curb and landed beside a can that had been set out for the garbage collector.

"Hey, that's neat."

"Yeah. But it makes me different, and people don't like kids who are different."

Jackson Jones nodded. "I know. They make fun of my eyes. I don't see what difference it makes, if one's blue and one's green. I can see out of both of them, and that's what counts."

"They make fun of you, but they aren't afraid of you," Katie said. "Mrs. M. says that's why people are cruel, because they're afraid of anybody who's different."

Jackson Jones sank down onto the top step. "I'm afraid I didn't come up with any very good ideas overnight," he confessed. "Even in this house, I couldn't keep people from noticing you forever. Maybe you should at least talk to your mom on the phone. Maybe she can think of some way to keep them from arresting you. She can probably get a lawyer for you. They don't put people in jail without a chance to talk to a lawyer."

"What good would that do, unless the lawyer could convince them I didn't hurt my grandma? And he wasn't there—nobody was there—so how can I prove anything?" Katie sat down beside him, watching the other girls

149

playing out in front. One of them had spotted the silvery beer can, and they were kicking it back and forth as if it were a ball. "Besides, I think they don't have to let kids have lawyers, only grownups. There was a boy at our school who kept running away and setting fires, and they put him in juvenile detention center. *He* didn't have a lawyer."

"Well, at least your mom would feel better, knowing you aren't hurt or anything. And Mrs. Michaelmas said to tell you she wants to talk to you, too, if I see you. The way she looked, I think maybe she knows I wasn't telling quite all of the truth."

Katie considered. "Maybe I could talk to *her*. If I talk to Monica, and she cries, she'll make me feel worse than I do already, and it won't do any good. I'm not going home if they're going to arrest me and put me in jail." She was so depressed she almost wished she *would* cry.

"What are you going to do, then?" Jackson Jones wanted to know. "I'd let you stay here, but Ma's sure to notice you sooner or later."

"I guess I'll go try to find those other kids," Katie told him and didn't remember until she saw his startled face that he didn't know about the others.

"You mean there are more kids like you? Can they do magic, too?"

"It isn't magic. I mean, I think it's telekinesis. And I don't know if the others can do it or not, but maybe they can. Oh!"

She broke off, because through the mist that obscured her vision Katie saw a figure coming along the street, on the other side. Or, rather, two figures. A tall boy with a big dog.

She reached into her pocket for her glasses. In her

eagerness, she forgot to push them on with her fingers, and she didn't notice that Jackson Jones allowed his mouth to fall open as the glasses settled comfortably, all by themselves, onto her nose.

It was the boy from the park, the one who might be Eric VanAllsburg, being dragged along by the huge Airedale, and Katie rose to her feet, wondering how to approach him without scaring him off again.

And right then, while her mind was occupied with something else, Mrs. Jones came out onto the porch and saw Katie with her glasses on. She put a hand to her mouth.

"Good heavens! It's the little girl the police are looking for!" she said.

But before Mrs. Jones could do anything about it, Katie fled down the steps.

13

SHE heard Jackson Jones calling after her, but Katie didn't stop. Her flight had been unthinking, propelled by sheer panic, and it was only when she began to feel winded that she realized she'd run in the opposite direction from the boy with the big dog, the boy who might be Eric.

She turned and looked back, hoping that by some miracle the boy had turned, too, and was approaching her. There was no one, however, no one at all. No one was chasing her.

Would Mrs. Jones call the police? Katie had to assume that she would, which meant that Katie would have to find a place to go, a place to hide. Yet she couldn't hide forever. Maybe she couldn't even hide for a day or two.

Jackson Jones thought she ought to contact her mother because Monica was worried about her. Only was she worried because she thought Katie was dangerous or because she wanted to protect her?

Katie's instinct was to keep on running, but she had a stitch in her side, and she was breathing heavily through her mouth. She couldn't run any more for a while. So, instead, she walked. She didn't take the bus, although she had a few coins left in her pocket, and eventually she came to a place where things looked familiar. She was only a block from Dale Casey's house.

Could he help her? Probably not, Katie decided; she didn't even think he would be home, but he was the only hope she had. If he really was like she was, and she was convinced that he was, then he would at least understand about her, and that was more than anyone else had ever done.

The Casey house sat in the middle of the block, looking normal and not at all frightening. Yet after the way Mrs. Casey had yelled, "Stop that child," at her husband, Katie was leery of approaching it again.

She stood, pressing a hand to her side, trying to think. And after a few minutes it occurred to her that a car was sitting in front of the house, the car Mr. Casey had driven up in when Katie was there.

Of course, that didn't prove anything. Some families had more than one car. But maybe the Caseys had come home early; maybe Dale was around.

Katie did something then that she'd never tried before. She reached out, with her mind, into that house. She didn't know what it was like, inside, nor where Dale would be if he were home. But she sent currents of air moving, air that would give the curtains and draperies a life of their own. If there were papers lying loose, they, too, would shift position. If she'd known which room Dale was in, she'd have flung a few small stones against the windows as well.

Dale had indicated that he could read minds. Could he read hers, from half a block away, if she tried very hard to catch his attention?

She stood there in the warm summer sunshine until her upper lip was beaded with perspiration. Lots of people had ESP; she knew that, she'd read about it often. So maybe if Dale had a little more than ordinary people, he would feel that she was there. She tried so hard that she squeezed her eyes shut and held her breath until it suddenly exploded in a small gasp when she couldn't hold it any longer.

Katie opened her eyes.

And there he was, coming out of the front door of the big house. He paused on the front steps, looking around very casually, as if he had come out for nothing more important than to see what the weather was like. And then, without looking at her at all, he crossed the street and started walking in Katie's general direction.

For a moment she thought it was just coincidence that he'd emerged from the house while she waited, because if he stayed on the far side of the street his path wouldn't cross hers. After a moment, though, she realized that he might be taking precautions, in case anyone was watching.

When he was almost opposite her, Katie turned and went around the corner, so that no one from the Casey house could possibly see her. And sure enough, a moment later she heard the padding of Dale's tennis shoes on the sidewalk behind her.

It made her feel peculiar to look into those silver eyes, so different from any she'd ever seen except for her own. Peculiar and excited, all at once.

"Boy," Dale said, "you're sure creating a ruckus. Do

you know they showed your picture on TV last night and told people to call the police if they saw you?"

Katie licked her lips. "Did they say what for?"

"No." He hesitated, then blurted out, "My mom called them. They just talked to her. They didn't send a police officer out to the house." He hesitated again before he added, "My dad picked up a piece of paper you dropped. It had some names on it, mine and two other ones." He pulled a crumpled slip out of his pocket and handed it to her. "The police wanted to know about it, but Dad couldn't remember what the names had been, except for mine. He doesn't know I have it."

Katie took the paper, although she didn't need it any more. She'd memorized the names, and it didn't tell her how to find Eric VanAllsburg.

"Did you read my mind?" she asked. "When I wanted you to come outside?"

For the first time she saw Dale grin. It made some of his freckles disappear into the creases. "Boy! You almost overdid it. With the wind, I mean. My dad was reading the Sunday paper, and it flew all over the room, and the financial section blew into the fireplace and burned up before he got to read it. And it knocked over a bud vase onto a letter Mom was writing and spilled water all over her desk. She thought maybe I did it." The grin faded. "I get blamed for everything like that, even if I don't do it at all."

"But you really heard me asking you to come out?" Katie was intrigued by that; it seemed a handy ability to have.

"Not heard you, exactly. I was alerted when the wind began to blow inside the house, because I used to do that sometimes, before I decided it caused more problems than it was worth. So then I sort of went looking for you, or whoever was causing the wind. You know, mentally. And I felt you waiting, somewhere close by."

"I don't know exactly why I did it," Katie confessed. "Except that I didn't know what else to do. Can you read the whole story in my mind, or shall I tell you about it?"

"It's easier if you tell me," Dale decided. "I can't read everybody's minds. I'm just learning, you know. It sort of makes my head ache to try too hard, or for too long."

So they walked over to the park, where the same old man was again feeding the pigeons, and they sat on the edge of the pool and talked.

It was strange and exciting to talk to Dale, because it was the first time in her life that Katie had felt able to admit to anything that came into her head without being afraid of the consequences.

And Dale, it was clear, was having the same experience.

"They've kicked me out of three schools," he admitted. "They said I was a disruptive influence. Actually, I didn't do anything to anybody who didn't do something to me first. I don't know why the other kids picked on me, except that they always made remarks about my funny eyes. And one day I realized that this kid was planning to trip me when I walked past him, so I thought how neat it would be if his milk carton tipped over in his lap right then, and thinking about it seemed to make it happen. So he forgot about tripping me. And after that, I always seemed to know if they were planning something mean, and I could counteract it. Only the teachers said I caused trouble. Anyway," he concluded, "I guess being kicked out of school isn't as bad as having the police after you because they think you killed your grandmother."

Katie was glad she'd found an understanding friend, but that didn't change her basic problem. She came back to it with a sigh.

"Do you think you could read Mr. C.'s mind and find out for sure what he intends to do about me? So I'd know if I could go home or not?"

Dale looked toward the fountain in the middle of the pool, and suddenly the water sprayed over his outstretched hand and arm, cooling them. When he put his hand back in his lap, the fountain returned to normal.

"Well, I could try. If people don't want to let anyone know what they're thinking, it's harder. Like I said, I'm just learning."

"Do you have to get close to him to do it?"

"It helps. I picked you up from half a block away, but that was probably because I was looking for you, and you were trying to send a message to me. This Mr. Cooper won't be trying to do that."

Katie was feeling very warm, and she decided to try Dale's technique with the fountain. It was actually quite easy to make the water blow over her in a fine, cooling mist.

"Can you send messages, the way I did to you, as well as read minds?"

Dale considered. "I don't know. I never tried it. There was never anybody to send a message to who wouldn't have thought he was going crazy."

"Try to send me a message now," Katie suggested.

So they sat there on the concrete edge of the pool, and both of them concentrated. And into Katie's mind, almost like the impressions she'd received from Lobo the cat, came an image. An image of food, steaming hot, and a glass of cold milk.

It reminded her that Mrs. Jones's pancakes had been eaten a long time ago, Katie swallowed. "I can almost smell the hamburgers," she said.

Dale grinned. "Me, too. With onions."

Katie nodded, but she knew there was something more important than eating at the moment. "If you could send me a message about the food, can you send a message to Eric? I think he saw me and realized I knew he had made the Frisbee act up; he was afraid of what I might do or say about it, so he hurried away. Can you reach him and tell him we're friends and that we need to get together?"

Dale shrugged. "I never tried it, but what do we have to lose? Tell me again what he looks like, as much detail as you can remember, and I'll think about that as well as the message."

So Katie told him, and Dale closed his eyes and tried to project his thoughts to the boy they had yet to meet. And on the off chance that she, too, might be able to use her mental powers in this way, Katie did the same thing.

After about ten minutes, they found they had to rest. "It sort of gives me a headache to try so hard," Dale admitted.

It was Katie who saw him coming and rose slowly to her feet, the electrical trickle of excitement somehow being communicated to Dale so that he, too, turned and stood up.

He came straight toward them, a tall dark-haired boy wearing glasses, carrying a white paper sack. He didn't have the dog this time, but otherwise he was the same as Katie had described. And behind the lenses of his glasses, his eyes were silver-colored.

"Are you Eric?" Katie asked tentatively, although she felt quite certain that he must be. The delicious aroma of hamburgers with onions wafted from the paper sack, and she knew they'd done it. She and Dale had called up this boy they'd been searching for.

Eric spoke slowly. "Then there are more like me. I always thought there must be." He handed Katie the sack, regarding her seriously with the silvery eyes. "I assume these are yours. How did you do it? Find me, and make me buy your lunch?"

"Dale did it, mostly," Katie volunteered. "I saw you here in the park, moving the Frisbee, and I guessed who you were; only I didn't know how to find you when you ran away. Dale can read minds, though, at least some of them, and he can send messages without speaking. Can you do that, too?"

"Not that I know of. I've concentrated more on not letting anybody know what I was thinking, instead of the other way around." Eric studied their faces, and particularly their eyes. "I wouldn't have run, if I'd been close enough to see you like this. I'm not telepathic enough to figure out what's going on, I'm sure of that. Is anybody going to explain?"

Katie dug into her pocket for coins and a crumpled dollar bill to pay for the lunch, then passed one of the foil-wrapped hamburgers to Dale. They ate them sitting on the edge of the fountain pool, taking turns talking. Eric wasn't eating, so he was the one who began.

"First I got this strong feeling I should come to the park," he said. "And then, after I decided maybe I ought to do it even if I didn't know why, I felt a compulsion to stop and buy two hamburgers with onions. It was crazy, but I did it anyhow."

Dale started to laugh. *I guess you can project as well as I can, Katie. I wasn't thinking about the food any more."*

"Who are we?" Eric asked. "I'd decided I must have been born on some other planet, maybe brought here in a flying saucer and left for human beings to raise. I thought maybe some day the aliens, my own people, would show up and ask me to rise up against normal humans, and I'd have to decide whether to do it or not."

Dale stopped chewing. "Would you go against humans? If you *were* an alien from outer space?"

Eric considered. His dark hair had fallen forward into his eyes, and Katie noted that he made it move back into place and smooth itself out without touching it or thinking about it.

"I hadn't decided. Mostly, they've been pretty good to me. My folks have, anyway, even if they don't understand me. I guess you don't think we're aliens?"

So they explained to him that they thought it had something to do with the dangerous drug their mothers had worked with, before any of them were born. Sometimes all three of them talked at the same time, but it didn't seem to matter. Nobody got confused. Katie had never felt so exhilarated in her life.

And then she remembered.

"The police are looking for me," she said. "They think I pushed my grandmother down the stairs. And Mr. C. moved into our apartment house to try to find out things about me. I don't know for sure if he *is* the police, but I'm afraid to go home until I find out."

"That shouldn't be too hard," Eric said. "If Dale can

read minds, we can just get close enough to him to find out what he has in mind."

"I can't read everybody's mind," Dale said, wiping his mouth on a paper napkin. He sounded apologetic. "But I can try. It does seem to help if I get close to them. Shall we go see what we can do?"

Katie drew in a long shaky breath. "All right," she agreed. "Let's go."

14

THERE was no police car in front of The Cedars Apartments this time. But they didn't take any chances. Katie led the way around the back, through the alley, and they crept up through the shrubbery to look around.

A few minutes later an unfamiliar vehicle pulled up, and when the people got out of it, Katie felt Dale's fingers digging into her arm. His whisper was more felt than heard.

"It's her! The other one, Kerri Lamont!"

The girl was about their age, and even smaller than Katie. She had dark curly hair and horn-rimmed glasses. As she stood on the sidewalk, waiting for her parents to get out of the car, she seemed to look right at the three children mostly hidden behind the little cedar and bonsai trees.

Mrs. Lamont was tall and thin and would have been pretty if her mouth hadn't looked as if it was always twisted crossly. "Come on, Kerri, they're waiting for us," she said.

Mr. Lamont was older than his wife, with a fringe of graying hair around a bald spot that he didn't bother to try to cover up, the way Mr. P. did. He wore work pants and a plaid shirt and heavy boots, and he looked just as cross as Mrs. Lamont.

"This still sounds crazy to me," he said. He had a very deep voice, that rumbled out of a stout chest. "Just because somebody else has got a kid as peculiar as ours, why do we have to come rushing over here right in the middle of the ballgame? Why couldn't we have waited until I found out how the last inning came out?"

The family group was moving toward the building. Katie and the boys remained frozen into position, and only Kerri seemed aware of them. She didn't say a thing, though. Katie knew they ought to try to send her a telepathic message, but between her own fear and excitement, she couldn't think of anything that made sense.

"I told you," Mrs. Lamont said, in a tone that sounded as if she said the same words often. "Monica called and said that Sandra Casey had found a note with Kerri's name on it, and Dale's, and another boy's. And it's just as I suspected, those other kids are as peculiar as Kerri is, and now Monica's little girl has disappeared, and we have to find out what's going on."

"Why?" Mr. Lamont asked, kicking at a rock on the sidewalk. "Is knowing about those kids going to make Kerri any different?"

They talked about Kerri as if she wasn't there, or was deaf and dumb. Didn't they know what it made a kid feel like to know she was considered a freak even by her own parents?

"You don't care about anything but your stupid ballgames," Mrs. Lamont said. She was close enough now so that Katie could really see how pinched her mouth was. "You don't care about what's best for your kids."

They were still arguing as they entered the building. And then the waiting trio heard Kerri's voice, soft but firm. "I forgot my handkerchief. I'll be up in a minute, Mother."

"Apartment 2-A," Mrs. Lamont told her, and then the door clicked softly shut.

Kerri didn't return to the car, however. She stood on the sidewalk, looking toward the shrubbery.

"Over here," Dale said in a voice like an old-time stage villain, and Kerri obediently came toward them.

She didn't seem surprised or uneasy, as Katie thought she might have under the circumstances. She looked directly into each face, evaluating first the boys and then Katie. Her voice was quiet and melodious.

"I got your letter. I was trying to figure out how to answer it when your mother called. They found blood in the kitchen, and they're afraid somebody kidnapped you or something."

Katie lifted the finger with the Band-Aid on it. "I cut myself on the lid of the tuna fish can, that's all. I wasn't kidnapped. They want to arrest me because they think I pushed my grandmother down the stairs."

Kerri's glasses rose, hovered, and settled more firmly on her small nose. "No, they don't. I mean, maybe somebody does, but that's not why the police are looking for you. Your mother called them because they thought something bad had happened to you. They suspect foul play."

Foul play? That meant someone had murdered her, didn't it? Katie felt a pang of regret if that was what Monica had been worrying about. Poor Monica.

164

"You mean they aren't going to arrest me?"

"No. They aren't even looking for you any more, because a Mrs. Jones called the police, so they know you're all right. That you've only run away, instead of being kidnapped."

"But Mr. C. is still here. That's his car, over there." Katie pointed. "And he's been asking questions about me, and he frightened Mrs. M. He wants me for something; he came here to find out about me. He didn't just happen to move in and bring nothing to cook in and nothing to eat but yogurt and peanut butter sandwiches."

Katie was feeling confused, and her words came out that way, too. But it didn't seem to bother Kerri.

"I don't know about him. But if you could all send me messages without speaking to me, we should be able to handle Mr. C., whoever he is."

Dale cleared his throat. "I can read minds, a little. We were thinking of getting close enough to Mr. C. to see if I could sort of listen in on him."

"He's up there now, with your mother," Kerri said. "And my parents. And I think they've called Dale's parents and probably Eric's mother, too. Whatever Mr. C. is here for, it concerns all of us. Not just Katie."

Katie stared at her, and then at the boys. Was that true? Has she misinterpreted what she'd overheard? Had Mr. C.'s questions not been a personal attack on Katie but an investigation into anyone who was able to do unusual things?

"I liked Mr. C., when he first came," she said slowly. "Only he pretended to be something he wasn't, and he tried to get Mrs. M. to talk about me, and I was afraid."

"I'm afraid a lot," Kerri confessed. "It's so hard to remember not to pick up your pencil without touching it when you've dropped it, and to use your hands to do simple things you can do perfectly well without them."

"Can you read minds?" Eric asked.

"No. But I can see in the dark," Kerri stated. "My father's always saying, *For heaven's sake, turn on a light in there! How do you expect to find anything in the dark?* And I can only move things without touching them if they're small."

"Me, too," Katie said, the electrical trickle of excitement in her veins making her tingle all over. "Only I'm getting stronger, I think. I moved one of those big rocks around the flower beds. I wonder if we all worked together, if we could move something bigger?"

For a moment they were all caught up in the idea, forgetting the problem with Mr. C. They looked around for a worthy project upon which to combine forces.

Miss K.'s light blue Pinto rolled into the parking lot, and Miss K. got out. By common, unspoken consent, the four crouched lower behind the shielding shrubs. And, unexpectedly, Mr. P. climbed out of the passenger side of the car, struggling with two heavy bags of groceries.

"I sure appreciate the lift," he told Miss K. "Listen, I've got the makings for a steak dinner here, if you'd like to join me."

"I don't think so, thanks," Miss K. said. She started walking briskly toward the front door of the apartment house, almost as if she were anxious to get away from him.

Dale's freckled face was pressed into the scratchy branches. "She forgot to set her parking brake," he said under his breath. "I'll bet all of us together could move her car. We could roll it right forward into the next parking slot."

"No," Katie said quickly. "It might roll all the way back out into the street, and I wouldn't want anything to happen to her car. Miss K.'s a very nice person. But *he* isn't."

"Maybe we could help him get his groceries inside," Eric suggested. "They look pretty heavy. Maybe he'd appreciate the help."

Katie didn't stop to think of all the things that Mr. P. already blamed her for. She never even thought about any possible consequences. It was so exciting to be working with three other kids as a team that she didn't try to stop them.

What happened next was as much a surprise to them as it was to Mr. Pollard. Well, almost as much, Katie amended, staring so hard she nearly fell through the bushes and out into plain view.

Because the bags that Mr. P. had been clutching as if they were very heavy had seemingly taken on a life and motion of their own. They plunged out of his arms and smashed themselves against the front door, which unfortunately was just closing behind Miss K.

Cans rolled in every direction, and a package of rice broke and spilled out across the sidewalk. A bottle of wine broke, too, sending a spreading stain on the cement. A white-wrapped meat package skidded away to the feet of a passing and astonished St. Bernard.

Mr. P. yelled in frustrated rage, and the St. Bernard, taking advantage of the circumstances, picked up the package and trotted down the street with it.

"Hey, you mangy mutt! Come back with my steak!"

Nobody was sure who, if anyone in particular, had caused one of Mr. P.'s cans to fly up in the air. They all saw it come down, though, and nobody was quick enough to change its path.

It hit Mr. P. squarely in the middle of his bald spot.

"Oh, crumb," Dale muttered, and began to back away on all fours. "Let's get out of here."

Eric said something, too, but it was lost in Mr. P.'s howl of anguish. The others were already following Dale's lead, but Katie's shirt front was caught on a rose bush. As she jerked it free, she heard Miss K. ask, "What happened? I'm sorry, I didn't mean to let the door swing shut in your face," and Mr. P.'s angry retort.

"It's that blasted kid again! She's around here somewhere, and even if the police have given up on her, I haven't! I'll fix her if it's the last thing I ever do!"

"Katie, come *on!*" Eric tugged on her arm. Her blouse came free, and Katie ran. They didn't rest until they had reached the alley, where they leaned, panting, against a row of garbage cans.

"I think," Kerri said in a small voice, "that we overdid it."

"Yeah. But we proved something, too, didn't we? That if we work together, we're stronger," Dale pointed out. "Just think what it would be like if we could all go to the same school."

"That would probably make it worse," Eric said. He'd hit his hand on something, and he wiped the blood off on his pants. "I mean, if the kids don't like *one* peculiar person, how would they react to four of us?"

Katie looked around at them, the circle of faces that were all different except that each had silver eyes behind thick glasses. "I feel better, though. Knowing I'm not the only one. And there could be more, couldn't there? Maybe we could find more of us, if we really tried."

Eric decided his wound wasn't worth worrying about

and stuck the hand in his pocket. "What do you suggest, that we run an ad in the paper? *Call this number if you have silver eyes and paranormal powers?*"

"No. But there must be something we could do. I don't want to go back to living the way I did before, feeling all by myself. I wonder," she speculated wistfully, "if my mother will like me a little bit better if she finds out I'm not the only one?"

Nobody answered that, and she wondered if the others had had the same problem as she had.

After a moment of silence, Katie pushed herself away from the garbage can and put as much strength into her voice as she could. "I guess," she said, "we'd better go see what we can find out about Mr. C."

They went up the back stairs, quietly, unwilling to meet Mr. P. or anyone else. Behind the door of apartment 2-A, they could hear voices, many voices, all talking at once and interrupting each other.

Of one accord, the other three stepped aside to let Dale close to the door.

"Can you tell anything?" Kerri whispered.

Dale shook his head. "No. I can't pick out Mr. C.'s thoughts at all. There are too many people, and they're too emotional. I think that makes it harder."

Katie hesitated, swallowed, then spoke with determination. If it was true that she wasn't wanted by the police, and she had the backing of her new friends, maybe they didn't need to read anybody's mind.

"Why don't we walk in," she said, touching the unlatched door with her fingertips. "Maybe they'll tell us what it's all about."

And that was what they did.

169

Monica gave a cry of relief and rushed across the living room to crush Katie in a tight hug.

"Darling! Where have you been? Why did you run away?"

"I didn't want to go to jail. I didn't hurt Grandma, really I didn't, and I thought they were going to put me in jail."

Monica's eyes were filled with tears. "We'd never let anyone do that, darling. Never."

Nathan appeared behind her. "You OK, kid? You aren't hurt?"

"No. I'm all right." Katie saw a blur of faces around the room; even Mrs. M. was there in one of her flowered muumuus, looking as if her hair had just barely survived a hurricane. "Are you all mad at me?"

"No, no," Monica said. "We only called the police because we thought something had happened to you. There was blood in the kitchen, and you aren't used to cities—little girls get in trouble all the time in cities. So we asked the television stations to run your picture, in case anyone had seen you. Oh, Katie, you scared me half to death!"

Katie looked past her mother to Mr. C., who was running a hand through his hair so that it stood up almost as wildly as Mrs. M.'s.

"He was asking questions about me. He said the Armbrusters thought I hurt Grandma, and I thought he intended to lock me up."

Mr. C. made a face. "I guess I bungled the whole thing. I didn't mean to scare you, Katie. I *was* asking questions, but not because I wanted to lock you up. I was trying to find out the truth so I could protect you. I'm not a policeman, I'm with the Institute of Psychic Phenomena."

Katie blinked. "What's that?"

He glanced at her companions, then back at Katie. "It's a place where we investigate children like you, and teach them. We're all learning together, actually. I guess I need to learn a lot, myself. About how to handle cases like this without frightening people, the way I did you, Katie."

She wasn't sure she liked being referred to as a "case." Katie shifted her weight uneasily. "You scared Mrs. M., and that scared me. I thought you were going to lock me up."

Mrs. M. nodded her shaggy head. "Yes, he did. You oughtn't to go around scaring people. Pretending to be a friend, and then being so nosey everybody guesses you aren't what you seem. I didn't tell him a thing, Katie. I didn't trust him." Her usually pleasant face was contorted in a scowl. "I still don't."

Mr. C. spread his hands in a gesture of helplessness. "All right. I admit it. I handled this badly. But you see, when there are people—particularly children—who have what we call paranormal powers, the ability to do things ordinary people can't do . . . well, most of them learn very quickly not to let other people know how different they are. They keep it a secret, hide it. And often the other people around them, parents and neighbors who love them, cover up, too. They're afraid of what will happen if it gets out that the kids can move things without touching them, create winds, read minds. That kind of thing."

Monica had a very peculiar expression on her face. "You've been telling us that Katie really *can* move things with the power of her mind. And these other children, they can do things like that, too?"

171

Katie saw that the other parents present wore similar expressions. Mr. C. had been talking to them, but it didn't appear that any of them had told him anything about their own children, even though they had all been disturbed about their unusual qualities.

"How did you know anything about me?" Katie asked slowly.

Mr. C. was eager to answer that. "One of your teachers read an article I'd written for a professional magazine, Katie," he said. "She wrote to tell me she thought you might be like the special children I work with at the Institute. I had a vacation coming, so I went to Delaney to meet you. Only your grandmother had died, and you had left town, so I had to settle for talking to the people who knew you. Some of them, like the Armbrusters, were hostile enough to make accusations against you. That's not too unusual. Mr. Pollard, right here in this building, has done the same thing. He's afraid of you, and he'd like to see you taken away from here."

He had turned so that he was addressing them all, the children, but also the parents, who waited in silence.

"I asked a lot of questions because I had to be sure that Katie *was* one of the special children. I get a lot of mail about people who are supposed to be able to do unusual things. And, frankly, a lot of them are fakes. Some of them are trying to make money by pretending to be able to talk with someone else's dead relatives, for instance. It's a field in which there are a lot of charlatans."

Nobody asked what a charlatan was. Katie already knew it was a person who pretended to be something he wasn't, usually in order to cheat someone else.

"Our school is for children who are genuinely blessed

with extraordinary powers," Mr. C. went on. "We want to help them learn how to develop their powers to the greatest extent. Katie was smart enough to figure out that there might be more of you, the ones who are here today, all born to mothers who worked with a dangerous drug. Well, of course *all* drugs are potentially dangerous; but this one was so dangerous it was discontinued by the manufacturer when he realized it could do real harm to the people who handled it. Sort of like being around when an atom bomb goes off."

He took a deep breath. "The drug didn't necessarily cause obvious trouble right *then*, but tests, even ten years ago, showed that its use could have serious consequences years later. Just the way it has had with these children. But in this case the results were not bad. The four of you have powers the rest of us don't have, powers that could be of immense value to the human race. We at the institute want to know what these powers are, and how they can be developed to produce the most good for the most people. I know from what Mr. Pollard and the others said that Katie, at least, can do some amazing things."

Katie stood there, neither denying nor admitting to anything. She still wasn't sure she trusted Mr. C., any more than Mrs. M. did. Nobody else was admitting anything, either.

"Look," Mr. C. said. "I know you've all had difficulties adjusting to going to school and living with ordinary people. Mrs. Michaelmas thought I should leave you alone to be a normal girl. But the thing is, Katie, you aren't normal. You're going to have more than the usual number of problems in growing up, and we think we can guide and help you with them."

It was true; she had always seemed to have more problems than most kids. Katie was intrigued at the thought that it might be possible to use her abilities openly. It would be nice not to have to watch her step every single minute, the way she'd been doing, or trying to do.

"Are there other kids at your school?" she asked. "Like us?"

"Yes. There are seventeen there now. We think there will be more, but it's hard to find them. They don't know about us, or they don't understand, and they try not to be found."

"Did their mothers all handle that drug before they were born?" Kerri asked.

"No. Only the mothers of you four children handled that particular drug, as far as we know. Some of the others were born to mothers who worked with other dangerous substances, and some of them are still a mystery to us. We don't know why those children have special talents. It's one of the things we're working to find out."

Dale spoke slowly. "We wouldn't be considered freaks at your school, would we?"

"We wouldn't have to remember not to do things that are perfectly natural to us," Kerri added, "so that people wouldn't think we were crazy. Sometimes people think I'm crazy, or a witch, or something." She sounded wistful.

"I promise you," Mr. C. said. "At our school nobody would consider you a witch or a freak."

Eric cleared his throat. "And what is it you want of Katie, and of us? Why were you investigating?"

"Because," Mr. C. said, "I would like very much for you all to come and live at our school. You'll like it there, I think." He smiled, but none of the children smiled back at him. Not yet. Try as she might, Katie could not read anything in his mind, couldn't tell how sincere he was. Did he want to help them, or only, in some way she didn't yet understand, to help himself? She didn't quite see what he would do for himself, but she was still getting used to the idea that he didn't want to put her in jail.

"Is there a wall around your school?" she asked thoughtfully.

"A wall? No. There's a fence, an ordinary fence, because the school is on a rather large estate, and we have our own farm animals that have to be kept in. It's a very pretty place."

"But not here? A long way off?"

Mr. C. smoothed down his hair. "About three hundred miles away," he admitted. "But you'd be with other kids like yourselves. Kids who would accept you the way you are."

It was Dale who put the next question. "Are they really like us? Do they have silver-colored eyes, too?"

"Well, no," Mr. C. said. "Actually, only you four have silver eyes, of all the children we've discovered so far. We may find others, of course."

Katie glanced at her mother. Monica had been so relieved to see her, Katie couldn't doubt that she'd been genuinely worried. Now Monica gave her a little smile, and it made something feel funny in Katie's middle.

"I want to know the other kids," Katie said slowly. "But if we're all kept apart, in a special school, won't we still be freaks? People know the kids at your school are different, don't they? Won't they still be afraid of us and suspicious of us?"

There was a silence, and Monica reached for Katie's

hand. "Katie's right. Children—at least young children—need to have a normal family life, don't they? Even if they are . . . special. They need to know their parents and brothers and sisters, don't they? And they need to be able to relate to other people, the people they'll eventually have to live with and deal with, unless they're going to be isolated from the rest of society forever. That's not what we want, is it?"

"They'd feel more at home in a school for kids like themselves," Mr. Casey said. "Wouldn't they? I know Dale doesn't fit into *his* school very well. It's hard for him to make friends among ordinary kids. And I'll have to admit it's been very uncomfortable for us, having a kid who's bright and different from anybody else's kids. We have to keep pretending to our friends that he *isn't* different."

"Mrs. Michaelmas is my friend," Katie said. "Even if she doesn't understand what I do, or how I do it. And Jackson Jones is my friend, too. He doesn't have special powers either, but he helped me. Maybe it would be better to learn to live with all the regular kind of people. Couldn't we do that, and go to the school, too? Only just part of the time? Not living there all the time?"

"The school is a long way from here, Katie," Mr. C. said gently.

"Well, there are four of us here," Eric spoke up. He shoved his glasses back up on his nose without ever touching them, just the way Katie was used to doing. "Why couldn't we live at home and have our own school? Sort of an extension school, the way the colleges do?"

Mrs. Casey gave a nervous laugh. "Yes, why not? We could tell people our children were in a special school, without telling them *how* it was special. Let's face it, the public in general is afraid of anyone who's different. Maybe the kids can handle it when they're grown up, but right now they can't, can they? Why couldn't we tell everybody they're in a school for especially bright children?"

"Even being in a school for slow learners would be easier to understand than the truth," Mrs. Lamont said. "Why *couldn't* we have a school here? I mean, they could go to the regular schools during the week, like the other kids do, and then on Saturdays, maybe, they could have special classes the way they do for the Gifted Children Program, where they learn Russian and advanced math and things like that. *Our* kids could learn— well, whatever they'd be learning at your school."

Kerri had a soft, sweet voice. "I think at Mr. C.'s school they want to study *us*. As if we were bugs."

"We *do* want to know more about you," Mr. C. admitted. "But not as if you were bugs, Kerri. You're special people, and you can probably be important leaders, or do things that will be of tremendous benefit to mankind, if you want to. We think we can help you do that, and also help you learn to be happy in a world that's mostly filled with people who may have to be taught how to accept your differences."

Katie felt Monica's fingers tighten on hers. "I think Eric's right, and Fern's idea is good, too," Monica said. "I can see that Katie does need to be with other children like herself, but I think she needs to learn to know ordinary kids, too. And we've lived apart for six years; we're just beginning to get acquainted with each other again. I'd like to keep Katie at home, at least for a few more years, until she's more grown up. Although I guess I'll leave it up to her, whether she wants to stay with me or go to your school."

"Well, I guess we're going to have to talk about this a bit," Mr. Casey said. "It's too important to make a decision without some serious consideration, Mr. Cooper. And, of course, the kids will have to have a big say in it, too. I think they'd better have a chance to get acquainted with each other, and maybe we could all visit your school before we decide what to do."

Katie could see that Mr. C. was disappointed that they didn't all agree at once to what he wanted. The idea of living in a place with a lot of kids like herself did make her sort of excited, but it was kind of scary, too. She glanced at the others, and she didn't need to be a mind reader to know that they all felt the same way about it.

Kerri's father cleared his throat loudly and asked, "What does this school cost? I mean, we're not rich people. We can't afford private schools."

All the grownups started talking at once, but Katie didn't listen to them. She looked at the other silver-eyed children, and by mutual consent, without any of them saying a thing, they all moved toward the door that led out onto the deck. Dale slid the patio doors closed on the noisy voices and joined the others at the railing, looking down over the swimming pool.

They hadn't had a chance to talk to each other very much, yet somehow they didn't seem to need to. Considering that they were all strangers, Katie felt remarkably comfortable with them.

"Could you tell?" she asked Dale. "Read Mr. C.'s mind? Is it on the level? Or is it like Kerri said? They want to study us like bugs?"

"A little of both, I think," Dale said thoughtfully. "I

mean, I think he's sincere in saying he wants what's best for us, and for everybody else. I don't know if we'd always agree with him that what *he* wants is what *we* want." Unexpectedly, he grinned. "I think it might not be too hard to pretend we were bugs under the microscope, and that we didn't understand what he wanted of us."

"Things would be a lot easier," Eric observed, "with four of us, than with each of us alone."

Nobody responded to that. They didn't have to.

They stood in a row, with their hands on the railing, and saw Mr. Pollard come out of the building with a towel and suntan lotion, and his newspaper. Miss Katzenburger was already there, in her electric blue bikini, and he walked up and said something to her.

Miss K. shook her head. Then Mr. P. put a hand on her arm, and Miss K. shook it off, as if she were irritated with him.

At that moment, Lobo started across the pool area. He didn't want to drink from the pool; the chlorine in it made it taste bad. Katie guessed he was only taking a short cut.

Then suddenly, from the corner where the door opened onto the area near the back alley, a familiar figure appeared. A big Airedale, sniffing around and lifting his head.

"Toby! He must have followed me again," Eric muttered, and started to move toward the stairs.

"Where did that mutt come from?" Mr. Pollard demanded. "Get out of here, you! Shoo!"

Toby didn't pay any attention to Mr. P. He took one look at Lobo and barked, a great deep bark that sent poor Lobo flying. The next thing the watchers saw was

Mr. P. kicking and yelling as the animals raced past him.

His suntan lotion sailed into the pool and so did his newspaper; and his towel wrapped itself around his head and face so that Mr. P. staggered, lost his balance, and went backward into the pool, shoes and all.

When he came to the surface, sputtering and choking and tearing away the sodden towel, Miss K. laughed. Toby and Lobo had disappeared, but Katie wasn't worried about Lobo. He could look out for himself.

Mr. P. looked up and saw the four children above on the deck.

His face got red, and so did his bald spot.

He made a savage grab for the pages of the newspaper before the sheets floated away or sank and threw the unreadable mess onto the tiles in front of Miss K. She was still laughing.

"There are four of them now," he said, his voice carrying clearly to the silent watchers. "There ought to be a law against kids like that."

"You aren't blaming them for your falling in the pool, are you?" Miss K. asked. "They weren't anywhere near you. You know, Mr. Pollard, if that little girl bothers you so much, why don't you consider moving? I have a friend who's looking for an apartment. The one you have would suit her just fine."

Mr. P. didn't answer. He started to climb out of the water, and as if the soaked newspaper had a life of its own, it suddenly rose from the tiles and plastered itself across the man's chest and face.

Katie hadn't done anything at all. She wasn't sure which of the others had. She simply waited to see what would happen, and in a way she could, almost, feel a little bit sorry for Mr. P.

"He doesn't pay the paper boy," Katie said softly.

"He hates dogs and cats," Eric added.

"He uses slugs in vending machines," Dale murmured.

"He uses nasty language," Kerri observed.

Just then Mr. P. reached for the floating bottle of suntan lotion; as his fingers began to close around it, the plastic container spurted away, sailing halfway across the pool.

With an oath, Mr. P. plunged after it, and Miss K. laughed again.

Above on the deck, Katie turned her head to look at Kerri, whose mouth widened in a secret smile.

Whether we go off to school or stay at home, we're going to have a lot of fun together.

Yes, Katie thought back.

And then they were all smiling, the same secret smile touching all four pair of silver eyes in the same way.

Whatever happened now, Katie thought, just for herself, she didn't believe she was ever going to be lonesome again.

And when she looked at Kerri and Dale and Eric, she knew they were thinking the same thing.

About the Author

Willo Davis Roberts is the author of a number of mystery and suspense novels for children and young adults. Her books include *The View from the Cherry Tree*, *Twisted Summer*, *Don't Hurt Laurie*, *Megan's Island*, *Baby-sitting Is a Dangerous Job*, *Hostage*, *The Girl with the Silver Eyes*, *The One Left Behind*, *Scared Stiff*, *Caught!*, *The Kidnappers*, and *Undercurrents*.

CURL UP WITH A GOOD MYSTERY!

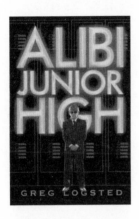

GOT FEAR?

MAKE SURE TO PICK UP ALL THE SPOOKTACULAR TITLES IN R.L. STINE'S GHOSTS OF FEAR STREET: TWICE TERRIFYING TALES SERIES

FROM ALADDIN
PUBLISHED BY SIMON & SCHUSTER